The Mystery of Ornate Mirrors

paranormal romance, Volume 1

Celeste Devine

Published by Michelle Smith, 2024.

THE MYSTERY OF ORNATE MIRRORS

First edition. November 22, 2024.

ISBN: 979-8230418665

Written by Celeste Devine.

Table of Contents

The Mystery
of
Ornate Mirrors

Magic Love

Celeste Devine

Copyright 2024 @ Celeste Devine

Acknowledgement

A HEARTFELT THANK YOU to Emily for her creativity and for inspiring me to continue exploring the wonderful world of paranormal romance. I hope you enjoy this series as much as I do and will become part of our romantic fantasy community.

Chapter One

The gentle cool summer breeze blew all around as Torvi Jones drove through the road leading to her late aunt's country house. It was almost noon on a bright Saturday, and she still hadn't arrived at her destination.

The house is located on the outskirts of the city. She had to drive the often-lonely road for over four hours from her apartment in the city before getting to the house.

Soft classical music played from her car stereo, but she wasn't in the mood for it; she wasn't in the mood for anything. Her love life and work at the advertising company hasn't been going well.

For over two years, she had worked tirelessly, putting in twice the effort of anyone else in the hopes of earning a promotion and joining the creative team at her company. Despite her dedication, her efforts remained unrewarded. She knew she had the creative imagination to contribute to the idea-creating board, but her boss seemed to have other plans.

She often thought about quitting but never found the courage to follow through. She believed in her abilities, knowing she was better than some of the creative advertisers in her company. Whenever a task was assigned, she would jot down ideas for the advertisements, but she was never given the chance to present them because it wasn't part of her job description.

She often cringed when ideas inferior to hers were accepted. She would stare at her notes in silence, masking her pain behind a forced smile. Her job consisted solely of recording meetings and schedules for everyone, and she was fed up with the same monotonous routine she repeated every single day.

Longing for something new, exciting, and out of the ordinary, she knew she deserved more out of life if only she could reach out and take it. Perhaps after her one-month vacation, she would finally muster the courage to leave.

A new determination settled over her as she drove along the quiet, peaceful road. If her boss dismissed her ideas again without listening, she would walk away and never look back. Her creative ideas were brilliant, capable of making any advertising company shine, and she was no longer willing to hold back her talents.

For now, she would let go of every unhappy thought and immerse herself in the beauty of her aunt's house. Nothing would stand in the way of her enjoying every moment to the fullest. Her problems would be the last thing on her mind during her one-month vacation. She needed this break, a chance to escape from it all and bask in the tranquility of being away from the city.

When the lawyers informed Torvi about her aunt's passing and the house she had inherited, she merely acknowledged the news and continued her mundane routine, never once considering visiting the property. Torvi felt a pang of sadness that Aunt Sonia didn't have a funeral. However, she understood that her aunt always did things her own way and disliked funerals, so it wasn't surprising.

She knew the house was beautiful, having spent much of her childhood there with her aunt. However, she believed it wouldn't be useful to her now, living in the bustling city and being consumed by her demanding job, despite how suffocating it felt.

With the frustrations at work and the recent heartbreak from her boyfriend of two years breaking up with her, the thought of inheriting a large, old house did nothing to excite her, despite the fond memories she had of it from her childhood.

Torvi had simply ignored the lawyers and never bothered to visit them to collect the house key and other documents. To her, her apartment was just fine, even though it wasn't as big or grand as her aunt's place.

After three months of silence the lawyers contacted her again. They informed her that the housekeeper, appointed by her late aunt to manage the property in the event of her passing, had resigned a couple of months ago. They emphasized that the house should not remain unoccupied for an extended period. If the house wasn't claimed or occupied within the next six months, it would be transferred to a charity organization to be sold. Torvi needed to sign some documents to officially become the new owner of the house.

This time, Torvi knew she couldn't ignore it any longer. Even though she didn't need the house right now, it had once been her second home. Deep down, she knew her aunt wouldn't want it sold to a stranger. Her aunt had always talked about wanting the house to stay within the family, passed down through generations.

She signed the necessary documents, collected the house keys, and embarked on her long-overdue vacation. With her car packed with clothes and groceries for the month, she set off with a renewed determination to take charge of her life and find all the happiness she could.

Torvi had always felt different. Often, she would look at others and sense there was something unique about her perspective. She saw life as a wonderful place, brimming with amazing things yet to be discovered, just like her aunt did.

Aunt Sonia was known as an eccentric old woman, and most of the family didn't understand her. However, she and Torvi shared a unique bond, and Torvi loved her aunt greatly. As a child, the time they spent together was always magical, creative, and special, an experience she never had anywhere else. There was also something about the house, a distinctive quality she couldn't pinpoint, but it was always there.

Torvi felt a surge of excitement as she approached the house. The air seemed different, with a gentle breeze drifting through her car and the melodious chirping of birds filling the trees.

The environment around the house was always lush and green, no matter the time of year. Torvi loved the vibrant flowers, fresh vegetables, and abundant vegetation. Aunt Sonia had a large, fenced flower garden where she grew different wildflowers that bloomed and filled the house with beautiful different scents.

Her excitement mounted as she got closer, and she smiled to herself, wishing she had agreed to come sooner. After a few more minutes, Torvi turned into her aunt's driveway. Although there were other country homes, cottages, and ranch houses in the region, Aunt Sonia's mansion stood out in all its grandeur, slightly isolated from the rest. The large glass windows gleamed in the afternoon sunlight, and white daffodils surrounded the house, their tall blooms nearly reaching the walls. Short stairs led to the impressive double doors, and the white-painted walls added to its magnificent appearance. The grounds were spacious, unlike the other houses around. It had a large area of land filled with trees that provided cool shade from the afternoon sun.

Upon arriving at the big black gate, Torvi parked the car and stepped out, stretching her long, slim frame. She wore a pair of black high-waisted trousers and a flowy, floral chiffon blouse. Her black high-knee boots accentuated her long, athletic legs.

Taking in the fresh, clean air, she removed the band she had used to hold her long curly blonde hair and shook it free. She loved the way the breeze blew around her face, making her feel like a child again.

With a delighted smile on her face, she reached into her jeans pocket and retrieved a bunch of keys. She inserted the right one for the gate and pushed it open. She stared, fascinated at the big old house in front of her.

She was surprised to see the house looking unchanged. It felt as if it were just yesterday that she had been running around the house, her laughter echoing through the air as she joyfully dug her hands into the rich soil, planting flowers and picking some to adorn the dining table.

Torvi walked to the flower garden beside the house and opened the small white gate. The flowers were as vibrant as they had been when her aunt was alive. She wondered how that was possible, given that no one had visited the house in two months.

"I've never seen anything so beautiful," she muttered, bending towards the flowers and inhaling their sweet, fresh fragrance. The familiar sensation from her childhood churned through her as she breathed in the full-blooming flowers.

After a while, she reluctantly left the garden and headed to the front door. She loved the garden dearly, but she knew she needed to explore the house itself. Besides, there would still be plenty of time for her to sit in the garden with a book and a glass of fresh orange juice.

All feelings of unhappiness had evaporated. A different ambiance surrounded her, and she basked in it. Everything felt magical. The soft breeze caressed her skin like a tender lover, while the sun's warm rays cascaded down, enveloping her in warmth. Even the air felt different. She could feel herself shaking off the old energy and embracing something new, pristine, and sensational. With her head held high, she closed her eyes, allowing the feeling to wash over her, reaching into her very soul. It was the same feeling she always had when spending time with her aunt as a child, but now it was much more profound and powerful.

Torvi allowed the memories of the happy days to wash over her as she climbed the steps leading to the big double doors with the heart shaped handles. As she inserted the key into the front door, she stared up at the roof, noticing how new and strong it looked despite the years.

She stepped into the large living room, designed to resemble a palace. It was extraordinarily spacious and was filled with her aunt's favorite paintings.

Aside from tending to her precious garden, Aunt Sonia loved to paint. Torvi remembered sitting on a stool in the garden for hours while her aunt worked with her brushes and canvas, capturing the natural elements around the house.

The walls were adorned with paintings of red roses about to bloom, large yellow daffodils swaying in the wind, the half-moon peeking through the clouds, and the bright, shining sun.

Torvi stared at the paintings with renewed interest, as if seeing them for the first time. Everything in the living room looked the same. The blue walls with their gold trimmings looked new and dust-free, the air was fresh, and there was no sign that the house had been uninhabited for months.

She placed her hands on her waist and gazed around with the eagerness and excitement of a child in a candy-filled house.

Although Aunt Sonia often invited the family to visit, they rarely ventured into her house. During the summer holidays, Torvi's parents would drop her off before heading off on vacation with her younger brother. On the rare occasions they did step inside, they always sat in a corner, looking uneasy as they curiously observed their surroundings. Torvi often tried to share the creative and magical atmosphere she felt in the house, but her family always seemed eager to leave.

Her parents were surprised when, after her first visit, Torvi wanted to spend every holiday at her aunt's house. They couldn't understand why Aunt Sonia chose to live alone in a large house far from the city. It seemed odd to them, and they never allowed themselves to be captivated by the house's essence or appreciate its serene beauty.

Her parents often asked what she and her aunt did to stay busy, but no matter how hard she tried to explain, they couldn't understand the connection she had with her aunt and the house. There was something about it that always made her feel cheerful, alive, and happy. At night, she and her aunt would sit on the front steps, watching shooting stars and munching on freshly cut fruit. Torvi couldn't remember ever feeling as content as she did back then.

At eighteen, Torvi went off to college, and her visits to her aunt began to decline. After college, she got caught up in adulthood and its many challenges. She had stopped visiting, though she still spoke with her aunt occasionally and saw her on trips to the city for bank transactions or legal matters.

Feelings of nostalgia washed through her as she stood there in the middle of the room, staring at all the beautiful pieces of furniture her aunt cherished so much. When she remembered how reluctant she had been to accept the house, she felt overwhelmed with remorse.

She had allowed herself to get so caught up in the bustling life outside that she forgot about the only place she had been truly content and happy. The house, with its gardens and trees, made her childhood special and filled with wonderful memories.

Tears rose to her eyes as she walked up to a framed picture of her and her aunt hanging on the wall. The photo, taken exactly twelve years ago, captured a summer day when she was thirteen, just blossoming into her teenage years. Her aunt had celebrated her birthday at the house, the only time every member of the family had been there together. The party lasted just two hours before everyone drove back to the city, leaving Torvi alone with her aunt in the vast house.

That night, Torvi and her aunt sat on the front steps, watching the full moon illuminate their surroundings. The air was peaceful, and they sat in companionable silence, basking in the serenity.

The beautiful memories made Torvi's heart ache with longing, wishing she could relive those moments with her aunt. She reached out and tenderly touched her aunt's face in the picture, feeling a deep connection.

"I'm sorry for being reluctant to accept the house at first, Aunt Sonia" she whispered, tears streaming down her cheeks. "Thank you for leaving it to me. It was so thoughtful, and I promise to always take care of it. I love you so much."

Relief washed over her as she finished speaking, as if she could sense her aunt's presence, reassuring her that everything would be just fine. She wiped her tears with the back of her hand and stepped away from the picture, a smile spreading across her face. It felt good to be back in the place where she had her fondest childhood memories.

Now it belonged to her, she could explore all the delights it held. There were many things she needed to see and lots of wonderful old books her aunt kept in her library she wanted to read. She stared at the stairs leading to the rooms upstairs and wondered where to begin her exploration from. After a moment of hesitation, she decided to explore upstairs first because she had never been to these rooms before.

Throughout all the time she spent with her aunt, Torvi had always stayed in the small room beside her aunt's large bedroom. Often, she would ask her aunt why they never used the rooms upstairs, but her aunt would only respond with a mysterious smile, promising that one day Torvi would get to explore them.

Everything they needed was downstairs; the library, kitchen, and her aunt's sewing and drawing room. Occasionally, Torvi would see her aunt going up the stairs with a knowing smile on her wise old face, and it aroused her curiosity, though she never dared to venture upstairs on her own.

Now, with the opportunity to explore, Torvi's heart pounded with excitement. Perhaps there was something special in the rooms upstairs, she couldn't wait to find out.

Slowly, she climbed the stairs, her eyes absorbing every tiny detail. At the top, a long corridor stretched out before her, with three rooms on either side, making six in total. Torvi stretched out both hands as she walked, touching each door and admiring the strong mahogany wood they were made of. Holding out her bunch of keys, she stared at them, wondering which one belonged to each door.

On closer inspection, she realized that each key had a tiny heart-shaped symbol with numbers one to six. These same numbers were also present on each door, indicating which key corresponded to which door.

Torvi studied the keys for a while before locating the number for the first door. The symbols were so tiny that they were almost imperceptible at first glance. The door to the first room squeaked as she turned the key and slowly pushed it open.

She paused midway into the room, captivated by the beautiful design and simple decorations. Like the rest of the house, it had a certain freshness that puzzled her; she couldn't fathom how a house could retain such a fresh smell despite being unoccupied for months.

Moving deeper into the room, Torvi's eyes fell on a large ornate mirror positioned in the center of the wall. It was long and spacious, occupying the entire middle section of the wall. The mirror had a beautiful wing-shaped frame adorned with intricate gold designs on both sides, giving it a sophisticated look, as though it belonged in a fairy tale.

Torvi's eyes widened in surprise as she studied every detail of the mirror, wondering where it had come from. She had never seen anything like it in her life. The mirror's surface was like a crystal and seemed to glimmer, as if the sun's rays were shining directly upon it.

Questions flooded her mind as she stared in awe at the unusual mirror. Had it been there all those years she spent in the house? Was this why Aunt Sonia never allowed her to venture into the upstairs rooms? Did her aunt want her to discover something about the mirror on her own after she was gone?

Torvi had no answers to her questions; the only person who could have provided them was gone. She realized she would have to figure out these mysteries by herself. Her intrigue with the mirror grew with every passing second, and she found herself increasingly enchanted by it.

She stared at her reflection in the mirror, performing a little ballet dance. She whirled on her toes, chuckling as her hair cascaded over her face. Suddenly, she felt a familiar tug at her heart, as if the mirror was calling out to her, beckoning her to step closer.

"Hello, big mirror," she called out softly, waving at her reflection. The mirror seemed to shake slightly in response, but Torvi couldn't be sure if it was real or just her imagination. Everything felt mesmerizing, and she never expected to find something so enchanting in her aunt's old house.

"Let's see what's in the next room," she whispered to herself, curiosity lighting up her face. The tug grew stronger, pulling her towards the mirror with an almost magnetic force. The feeling intensified; like something was calling her from the mirror, wanting to pull her closer and closer until she was deep inside of it. She stared intently at the mirror, searching for anything extraordinary about it.

Torvi convinced herself that apart from its elaborate beauty and sophistication, there was nothing more to the mirror. Perhaps it was the thrill of discovering something new in the house or the magical atmosphere, but whatever it was, she was determined to explore every room and have a great time doing it.

Waving away the feeling, she went out of the room and closed the door behind her. At the second door, she studied the heart-shaped symbol on it for a while then selected the key with the same number.

Pushing the door open, she stepped cautiously into the room. Torvi stood frozen when she saw the second mirror in the second room. She had thought the one in the first room was the only one, but she was wrong. Although it was as large as the first mirror, this one was triangular with a thick frame. It was adorned with paintings of tails and scales, and embedded with emeralds, giving it a distinct appearance.

She walked quickly towards it, her eyes surveying every bit of it. Again, she stared at her reflection in it, looking into her deep blue eyes and full round lips. Seeing the mirrors in the rooms was surprising; she had never thought it would be possible to come across something like it.

To her shock, the familiar feeling of being drawn to the mirror started all over again, the pull much stronger than before.

"What's happening?" she asked her reflection, hoping for an answer, but only her voice echoed back in the silence.

She left the second room, curiosity gnawing at her. What was in these mirrors? Was there something her aunt wanted her to discover? A secret the world didn't know about, or was it all in her head?

"No," she muttered, shaking her head as she inserted another key into the third door and pushed it open. She was certain she wasn't imagining it. There was no way she could have imagined the same thing twice. The feeling of being drawn to each mirror was real and strong.

Torvi eagerly checked the remaining four rooms, wondering if they all had mirrors. Each room did, and each mirror was exquisite and unique, astounding her.

The mirrors captivated her, tugging at her, urging her to enter them. She couldn't begin to understand why. Trying to process what she had seen, she decided to investigate each room again in order. She returned to the first room, her eyes quickly finding the mirror in the middle of the wall, just like in the other rooms.

This time, she tried to see if the mirror was installed on the wall, but there was no sign of installation. It seemed as though the mirror was part of the wall itself. She placed her hands on the wall, feeling for the mirror's edge, but her hands met only the wall. There was no indication it had been fixed by someone.

Torvi's excitement grew as she felt the familiar tug again, each stronger than the last. With her heart pounding, she stretched out her hand to the mirror, but just as she was about to touch it, she quickly pulled back and tucked her hand into her jeans pocket.

She was scared. She couldn't predict what would happen if she touched the mirror, and the fear of something bad happening kept her from doing so.

Deep inside, she wanted to explore the mirror, to uncover what awaited her within, but she lacked the courage to do so at that moment. She didn't know what to expect, yet the uncertainty fueled her curiosity.

She headed back downstairs and settled on the living room couch, attempting to distract herself with other activities. However, the mirrors in the upstairs rooms continued to beckon her.

Standing beside a large picture frame of her aunt, she stared intently at it, pondering how her aunt had rooms built with such elaborate mirrors. Although she and her aunt talked about everything, she had never mentioned the mirrors. Had they suddenly appeared after her aunt's death? How could such rare mirrors just materialize, ones she had never seen anywhere else in the house?

As the thoughts swirled in her mind, the urge to investigate grew stronger. Torvi found herself climbing the stairs back to the rooms. Stopping at the first room, she hesitated before inserting the key and turning it.

She paused at the door, skeptical about approaching the mirror again. After a moment, she took one courageous step after another until she stood directly in front of it.

Torvi inched closer to the mirror, her face almost touching it. Fear and courage battled within her, and just as fear seemed to prevail, her courage surged. She slowly lifted her hand to touch the mirror.

On impulse, she cupped her hand to her lips and blew softly onto the mirror. To her amazement, a glow appeared in the center, illuminating the room with a shining blue light.

"Wow!" she gasped, blinking in disbelief at the mystery before her.

Tempted to step back, she instead chose to act on her courage and moved even closer. Her heart pounded with anticipation as she took several deep, calming breaths.

She didn't know what would happen if she touched the mirror, but she was certain it would be extraordinary. The glowing light illuminated her face, and she saw her eyes glowing as she stared at her reflection.

"Torvi, you've got this," she whispered to herself, closing her eyes briefly.

Carefully, she dipped a finger into the center of the mirror and watched in awe as it disappeared, as though the mirror was some kind of portal. Quickly, she pulled her finger back and stared at it, shocked to see a blue glow around it that soon faded.

"There's no going back now," she said bravely, stretching out both hands toward the mirror.

As her hands touched the mirror, they quickly vanished into it. Without hesitation, she stepped forward, and soon her entire body disappeared into the mirror. The glow intensified, filling the entire room with brilliant light.

Chapter Two

Torvi felt strange as she slowly opened her eyes and moved her body. Quickly, she turned to look around her, her face filled with confusion as she took in her new environment. She was standing in a forest surrounded by large oak trees and wild green grasses.

Turning to look behind her, she was surprised to find herself under the shade of one of the giant oak trees. Her eyes fell on the large ornate mirror behind her, and she stood still in shock. It was the same mirror from her aunt's house, but now she was in a different place. She could see a glow in the middle of the mirror and an opening that looked like a door. She looked ahead and gasped in surprise at what she saw.

In the distance, a city shimmered as if encircled by flames. Captivated, she took a few cautious steps and concealed herself behind another tree to get a better view. From her vantage point, she could see a magnificent silver gate leading into the city. She could hear faint voices in the distance but couldn't make out any words.

"This is the most beautiful place I've ever seen!" she gasped; her blue eyes wide with shock as she gazed at the city. "Where am I? Am I in some kind of magic world or something?" she wondered aloud, looking around in awe.

Her eyes returned to the mirror in the oak tree, and realization began to dawn on her. She ran back towards the mirror and peered into it. She could see the first room in her aunt's house. It became clear she had been transported to another world, a beautiful, opulent world with a city that glowed so brightly she had to squint to see it properly.

"Whoa!" she yelled, spinning around in excitement until her head began to spin and she felt dizzy. A twinge in her legs caused her to fall face-first on the grass, her hands spread out as she drew in deep breaths.

Suddenly, she heard voices approaching and quickly stood up, hiding behind a nearby tree just in time to see a group of five men walking in single file. They wore tight leather outfits that clung to their muscular frames, with swords hanging at their sides.

Tall and broad-shouldered, their bulging biceps caught Torvi's eye, and she couldn't help but stare in awe. As the last man passed, she accidentally stepped on a twig, producing a sharp crack. The last man spun around, his eyes locking onto the tree where Torvi was concealed.

"Caden, why are you stopping now?" one of the men in the front called out, a note of impatience in his voice.

"Just a minute Justin. I thought I heard something, some kind of sound," Caden responded, walking towards Torvi, his sword pulled out in front of him.

Torvi's heart pounded as the footsteps got closer. She quickly turned her back to the tree and folded her arms, not wanting to be seen by the men. She didn't know who they were, but from their uniformed outfits and swords, she could tell that they were some kind of guards or soldiers of the city.

She wondered what would happen if they discovered her at that moment. Would they take her to the city's ruler? Or lock her up somewhere once they realized she isn't part of them? She had caught a glimpse of the man's face before turning away, his eyes had a red gleam, like fire.

As the footsteps drew closer, Torvi's heart pounded harder. She wrapped her arms around herself, bracing for discovery. But just as he was about to look behind the tree where she hid, he turned back and walked towards the others.

Justin saw Caden walking back to the group. "You've only succeeded in wasting precious time," Justin stated, annoyance in his voice.

"You could have simply gone ahead without me," Caden responded, equally annoyed. "I am only following orders from the master."

Justin didn't say another word. Instead, he turned his attention to the path ahead of them.

Caden also joined the file, and they continued their walk back to the city. Just as they were turning toward the part which would take them back to the city gates, he turned back and stared thoughtfully at the oak trees.

He could swear that he had heard a noise back there, as though someone was hiding or something else was there. He hoped he was wrong though. Master Raul's order was clear: no outsiders were allowed into the city.

Torvi breathed a huge sigh of relief as the footsteps receded. She stepped out from behind the oak tree and peeked at the retreating figures, watching as they walked into the city gate in single file.

From the little conversation she heard between the two men, she was certain they were soldiers, working on some order from the master of the city. It was obvious there was some kind of rule about preventing strangers from another world from coming into their world.

Torvi walked back towards the first oak tree she had been leaning against when she arrived. She stared at the mirror thoughtfully, wondering if she should go back.

"No," she said to herself, shaking her head from side to side. "I can't go back now; it would be a waste if I go back without getting to explore the city."

Determined to go into the city no matter what, she looked around for something to conceal the mirror so no attention would be drawn to it. She looked around the trees for a few minutes when her eyes fell on a large green cloak to her left. She looked at it curiously, wondering how it got there.

"Perhaps someone dropped it," she muttered, looking all around her.

Quickly, she picked it up and attached it to the branches of the tree where the mirror was, covering it from view. She stayed watching the tree for a few more minutes before beginning her descent to the path the guards had followed earlier.

As she walked the path that would lead her into the city, Torvi felt unsure of what she would encounter, but she was determined to find out anyway.

The city glowed brighter and brighter as she got closer to it. Before stepping through the large gates, she looked around carefully, not wanting to draw unnecessary attention to herself.

She arranged her hair in such a way that it covered part of her face; from what she'd seen back at the oak trees, the guards looked the same way everyone back in her world did, except for the red gleam in their eyes.

"CITY OF UNUTILIZED MAGIC" was written in large, shining letters on the gates as she walked in.

"City of Unutilized Magic?" Torvi muttered to herself, puzzled by the name.

She was certain that the city's inhabitants possessed some form of magic, judging by the gleaming surroundings, but the name left her curious. She couldn't wait to discover what it meant and what kind of magic the people could perform.

People bustled about in torrents, their loud, excited voices filling the air as she passed by. Torvi averted her gaze, avoiding eye contact with anyone. She paid close attention to the people around her and noticed they had the same red glimmer in their hands. Earlier, she had been too preoccupied with hiding to see the red glimmer in the guards' hands as they passed through the oak trees. Quickly, she tucked her hands into the pockets of her jeans, careful not to reveal any part of them. Some people gave her curious stares as she passed, while others merely glanced at her before looking away.

The houses varied in size, ranging from modest to grandiose, yet they all shared a common feature: they sparkled. Torvi observed that some houses sparkled more intensely than others, though she couldn't guess why.

At the heart of the city stood three magnificent castles, their brilliance surpassing that of the surrounding houses. The central castle, in particular, gleamed like a diamond.

Fascinated, Torvi halted, her eyes widening at the sight of the most extraordinary castles she had ever seen. While the gates of the other two castles glowed with a red hue, the central castle had an additional shimmer, and its gates were crafted from exquisite, transparent diamonds.

She had never encountered anything like it, not even in movies or magazines. Her mouth hung open in admiration, unable to tear her gaze away. The entire scene mesmerized her, and an intense longing to see the castle's interior gripped her instantly.

"Stunning, right? I haven't been able to stop staring at it myself since it appeared three moons ago," a voice said beside Torvi, making her heart jump.

"Oh yes, it's stunning," Torvi answered quickly, keeping her gaze fixed on the house to avoid making eye contact.

From the corner of her eye, she observed the woman standing beside her. She was tall and lanky, with long trousers and a black hood draping over her lean frame, making her appear larger. Her short, dark hair stopped just at her shoulders, and like the others Torvi had seen, she had a gleam in her eyes and hands.

Torvi guessed they might be around the same age, but she couldn't be sure, given the magical nature of the place.

"I'm Annabel, but my friends call me Ann," the girl said, turning to briefly glance at Torvi.

"I'm Torvi," she responded, glad that Annabel had not extended her hand to her for a handshake. If she had, she would have instantly noticed that Torvi's hands didn't glow like the others. Torvi wasn't sure how Annabel would react to that. She seemed to have an easygoing personality, the kind of person Torvi would love to be friends with, but she wasn't ready to reveal her secret just yet. She needed to be sure she could trust her.

"Master Raul's magic powers grow with each passing day, and he never tires of buying more as long as there's a willing seller," Ann muttered, an angry look on her face as she pointed to the middle castle.

"He buys magic?" Torvi asked, too stunned by Ann's revelation to remember that she ought not to give herself away yet.

"You didn't know?" Ann inquired, her eyes widening with surprise as she turned to look at Torvi.

"Of course I know," Torvi chuckled nervously, trying to hide her unease. "I just thought he had stopped, considering how mighty his castle is," she lied, hoping it sounded convincing.

"Master Raul stopped? That's never happening" Ann scoffed. "He's not stopping until the magic of the whole city and even unborn children belong to him!"

Torvi's heart skipped a beat as Ann drew closer, cupped her hands, and whispered into her ear, "I hear that he wants his handsome son to marry the Fire Princess, all so he could tap into her magic."

Torvi made a loud believable gasp. She didn't know who Master Raul was, nor did she know the Fire Princess, but she had to act as though she did. The more time she spent with Ann, the greater the risk of exposing herself. She needed an excuse to leave.

"Uh, I better get going now. See you around," Torvi said, starting to walk away.

"My house is at the end on your right, just as you reach the edge of the city. Feel free to call in anytime, Torvi, and you can call me Ann!" Ann called out after her, the wind scattering her words in all directions.

WITHIN THE CENTRAL castle, Zac paced the expansive living room, his eyes occasionally drifting to his father, Raul, who sat unperturbed on a huge throne chair, exuding calm authority.

The living room was adorned with the finest pure gold sculptures, and glittering oil paintings of various wildlife. The walls were made of precious stones, and the floor, crafted from transparent diamonds, sparkled as Zac paced back and forth.

He wore a long red coat over black leather trousers, and his long black boots made a distinct tap-tap sound on the floor. His black hair, nearly reaching his shoulders, was braided and tied with a band. Zac had a fierce red glow in his eyes, the intensity deepening as he glanced at his father. A long sword hung from his belt, almost touching the floor, and his hands glowed with the same fiery red glow as his eyes. He abruptly stopped pacing and stepped closer to his father, his face contorted with anger.

"Father!" he said sharply, his voice trembling with fury. "You cannot force me to do things against my will. I am a man, and I make my own choices!"

Raul leaned back in his chair, a smug grin spreading across his face. "Well, Zac, this decision has already been made for you," he replied nonchalantly.

"There's no way I am marrying Fiya, the Fire Princess!" Zac thundered, his chest heaving. "You know all too well how much I despise her."

Raul's grin vanished, and rage instantly replaced it. His face mirrored his son's, only much older. "I don't care how you feel!" he growled, springing up from his chair. "With Fiya's firepower and the others I've accumulated, our household will grow tremendously stronger. I can easily take out the other masters, making me the sole ruler of this city, and eventually, of course, I'll pass it down to you."

"If you're so interested in her powers, why don't you marry her yourself, father? It would save us all a lot of headaches and arguments," Zac suggested, stepping toward his father.

"It is impossible!" Raul boomed, his deep voice resonating through every part of the room. "The magic of possession requires a male and female who haven't birthed a child before."

"Then count me out!" Zac yelled, his fury returning a thousandfold. "The powers, the wealth, and everything else - I don't care about your greedy ambition to outdo the other masters, Father. I am not going to sit still and watch you ruin my life because of your..."

"Shut up!" Raul roared, cutting Zac off. The veins in his neck bulged as he walked closer to Zac until they stood face to face, their noses almost touching as they stared each other down. Both were tall and broad-shouldered, but Zac was dark-haired, a trait he inherited from his mother, while Raul had long, silver hair.

Father and son stood locked in a staring contest until Zac finally backed down and looked away.

"Listen, son, you are going to marry Fiya, and that's an order. I won't have you disobeying me. I am your father, and you will do as I say," Raul said in a fierce whisper.

"What if I don't, Father?" Zac challenged, locking eyes with Raul. "What will you do if I disobey you and refuse to marry her?"

"Are you challenging me right now?" Raul inquired heatedly.

"Yes, I want to know what you would do if I didn't fulfill your selfish desires."

Raul threw his head back and let out a hoot of laughter, his whole body shaking. "You think you have enough power to challenge me? Don't forget, I knew everything before you were even born, Zac."

"I don't care Father. You have no right to choose a woman for me. I am not going to go ahead with the engagement or any other plans you've made."

Raul took a few steps away, sat down on his enormous chair, and the grin returned to his face as he stared at Zac. "You know how ruthless I am; you've seen how I deal with those who disobey me. Family is no exception Zac. I will strip you of all your privileges and disown you publicly. You'll be thrown to the streets without a single penny to your name."

"Is that all you can do, Father?" Zac chuckled bitterly, shaking his head. "Do you think I can't make a decent living on my own? You know how hardworking I am. Nothing you say or do will force me into marrying Fiya, and that's final."

"Don't push your luck, son. I will make you burn!" Raul threatened, his hands clenched in anger.

Zac was about to give a sharp retort when the door opened, and a young guard approached Raul to whisper something in his ear.

"Bring them in," Raul commanded eagerly.

The door flew open, and the five city guardians entered, looking formidable in their black leather outfits. Zac immediately stepped away from his father and moved to one of the smaller chairs.

Raul managed to contain his anger and nodded to the guest, signaling him to report on their survey of the land earlier that day. Caden, the leader of the guards, stepped forward and bowed low before Raul.

"Master, we have searched all around as you instructed," Caden began, glancing at the others as he continued. "We combed the forest surrounding the city and went as far as the caves at the boundary, but no one was there."

"Are you sure you didn't overlook any sounds or signs?" Raul inquired, his eyes drifting from Caden to the other guards.

Caden hesitated. He wanted to mention the sound he heard near the oak trees, but he could feel his colleagues' eyes drilling into him from behind. Reporting it would make the master question their competence, and besides, it could have just been an animal. Incurring the master's wrath for nothing wasn't worth it.

"No, master," Caden replied.

"Good, good," Raul nodded, looking pleased. "I need you to keep an eye on everyone in the city and report anything or anyone you find suspicious. You may leave now."

The guards bowed one last time and exited the room the same way they came.

"You see, son, all my plans are falling into place. I had a fretful dream about an external presence coming to ruin everything. The magic of possession would backfire if there was anyone from outside the city here. However, it must have been my worried mind conjuring things up. Now, I won't have a son I sired from my loins be the one to make my plans fail! You must marry Fiya. I will announce the engagement soon, and on the day you both join hands in marriage, I will begin my possession magic."

"I will allow you to wallow in your disillusion, father," Zac sneered, getting up from his chair. "This is the last time I am going to say this to you. I am not marrying her, you can't force me, and that's final!"

With that, Zac strode out of the room, taking the stairs two at a time until he reached his door. Kicking it open, he collapsed onto his large bed, plotting how to thwart his father's plan. The argument had drained him, and he was so angry that his hands shook. They had everything - gold, fame, and influence. Their castle was the most luxurious of all the master's castles. He couldn't understand why his father wasn't content with all they had.

Zac knew his father's threats were not merely words; they would be carried out swiftly. Yet, he remained unafraid. He believed deeply in passionate love and refused to deprive himself of experiencing true love by marrying a woman for whom he felt only contempt.

THE MORE TORVI EXPLORED the city, the more captivated she became by everything she saw. As she walked through the bustling streets, she noticed a tall building with "MAGIC ACTS" written broadly in shining letters at the top.

Approaching the entrance, she could hear cheers and laughter from inside. She decided she wasn't going to hide anymore; she would open up and learn as much as she could about the people before returning.

Pausing at the doorway, she surveyed the scene before her. People sat in fancy chairs, sipping drinks from long golden cups, and watching a variety of magic performances on a huge stage.

Torvi stared in awe as she watched a young boy transform into a cat and leap around the room, drawing admiration from everyone. Another young girl with black curly hair climbed onto the stage and clasped her hands together; they gleamed just like the others in the room.

The girl twisted her hands, and to Torvi's astonishment, a large body of water appeared in her palms. She sent it flying towards the spectators, who clapped excitedly.

"Who are all these magical people?" she muttered to herself, turning to observe the crowd around her.

She looked up just in time to see a drink being placed in front of her by a young woman dressed in a short black dress. Her eyes fell on the girl's hand, and she stared in confusion when she noticed that it didn't have a gleam or shine to it; it was just like hers.

"I sold my magic; I needed the money," the girl said, answering Torvi's unspoken question.

"Oh, I'm sorry about that," Torvi replied, staring up at the girl.

The girl's eyes opened in shock as she stared at Torvi.

"Come with me," she whispered, whisking Torvi out of the room and through a backdoor that led to a tiny bathroom. She peeked outside for a moment before firmly locking the door behind them.

"You are not part of us; what's your name, and where did you come from?" she gasped, coming towards Torvi and looking her all over.

"My name is Torvi, and I came through a mirror from my wall," Torvi answered, intrigued by the girl's gleaming red eyes.

"You're from the real world!" she exclaimed, shock in her eyes as she touched Torvi.

"Yes, where is this place? Which world is this, and why does everyone have magic, and why did you sell yours?" Torvi asked all at once, eager to know about the place she found herself.

"I'll tell you everything, but first, I need to find a disguise for you," Helena said, as she walked through the door.

"Wait!" Torvi called, grabbing Helena's hand. "I've been hiding my eyes and hands since I arrived, but I thought it would be nice to let myself be seen."

"It could be dangerous. You'll attract attention, and some people might want to harm you. You need to be certain of anyone before revealing yourself to them," Helena cautioned.

"But why would anyone want to harm me?" Torvi asked, incredulously.

"Something's happening in the city. I don't have much time, and I need to get you a disguise before people notice my absence. Stay put; I'll be right back," Helena replied.

"You didn't tell me your name."

"I'm Helena, now don't move."

Before Torvi could say another word, Helena was gone. She stared at the closed door and decided to wait. Her eyes wandered over the bathroom walls, admiring how smooth and shiny they were.

Different questions whirled through her head, and she couldn't wait to have them answered. Soon, the door flew open, and Helena came back with a small bag across her shoulders.

"Here, wear this," Helena said, pulling out a pair of glasses made from blue diamonds.

"Where did you get these so quickly?" Torvi asked, picking up the glasses and staring at them in fascination.

"These will hide your eyes while you're wearing them," Helena explained.

"Our parents left my brother and I a lot of diamonds before they died. I had to make these glasses from those diamonds before my brother could gamble them all away," Helena said, her eyes sad and wistful.

"I don't understand; people die here?" Torvi asked, sounding confused. "I thought you were all magical people?"

"There's a lot I have to explain to you, Torvi, but now is not the time. Don't worry about your hands; lots of folks like me who sold their magic don't have gleaming hands. But you must protect your eyes at all costs; you can't let everyone know who you are."

"Wait a while after I leave before you return to the showroom. When the moon appears in the sky, come back here and wait for me. I'll tell you everything about this city," Helena said, getting ready to leave.

"Please don't go yet," Torvi called as Helena moved to open the door. "I wanted to know what your magic was before you sold it."

"I had the magic of light; I could create light in the darkest of places. Selling it is something I regret every day, but I had no choice. I hope to get it back someday," Helena answered, tears filling her eyes, which she quickly blinked away.

"See you around, Torvi. Try not to attract too much attention to yourself." She smiled softly before walking out the door.

Torvi felt sad at the regretful look on Helena's face. She wished there was something she could do to restore Helena's powers, but she was merely a visitor in this unfamiliar place.

Tentatively, she placed the glasses on her face, surprised by their lightness. She waited for a few more minutes before stepping out of the bathroom and following the path Helena had taken.

Back in the showroom, Torvi tried to act naturally as she found her way to her seat. She locked eyes with Helena, who was serving drinks at a table near the door, and they exchanged a brief nod.

Turning her attention back to the stage, Torvi watched transfixed as a man with long, shaggy blonde hair replicated himself into ten different figures, all dancing to the music blaring from the loudspeakers. It was one of the most intriguing things she had ever seen, and she cheered and clapped along with the rest of the audience.

Out of the corner of her eye, Torvi observed Helena moving swiftly and gracefully from table to table, serving drinks. She imagined how Helena looked wielding her magic of light, creating and manipulating lightning with her hands. She wondered what had driven Helena to sell off her magic, unable to forget the sadness in her eyes as she spoke about it.

Her eyes scanned every face in the room, hoping to catch a glimpse of Ann, but she couldn't see her. She wondered what would have happened if she had revealed herself to her. From the little she had noticed about Ann, she seemed like a free-spirited person, and Torvi had no doubt she would be elated to know that she was from another world.

"My house is the last at the end of the city." Ann's words echoed in Torvi's mind.

She looked around the room and noticed another man had taken the stage, preparing to display his magic. It was clear to her that most people in the room were there to showcase their powers, and it would be a while before the event finished.

Deciding to pay a quick visit to Ann and return in time to meet Helena back at the showroom, Torvi rose from her chair and began descending the stairs to outside. A loud cheer erupted from the room, and Torvi whirled around to take one more glance at the performance.

She missed her step and slipped. Helena's glasses flew off her face, and Torvi lunged after them, her heart pounding in terror at the thought of the precious glasses shattering into tiny pieces.

Just as the glasses were about to hit the ground, a man dived down and caught them. His arms also encircled Torvi just in time to prevent her from falling. He cradled her head against his broad chest and steadied her on her feet.

Torvi opened her eyes in awe and looked into the most handsome face she had ever seen. She stared at his glowing red eyes and felt her heart race wildly in her chest.

24

Chapter Three

Torvi locked eyes with the man and suddenly felt faint, as though he consumed all the air around her. She wondered why he stared at her with so much shock, his mouth hanging open.

It took her a moment to remember that Helena's glasses were no longer on her face, leaving her eyes exposed. Fear gripped her heart as she wondered if he would be a friend or foe. Would he expose her to the others or take her to the master Ann and Helena had spoken about?

Quickly, she disentangled herself from his arms and took a few steps back. She tried to avoid his gaze, but she couldn't help herself. He hadn't moved an inch, still staring at her, spellbound and shocked.

Torvi cleared her throat softly and glanced around, wondering if anyone was paying attention to them. Aside from a few curious glances at the man, everyone seemed to be going about their business.

"Uh, can I please have those back?" she asked, trying to snatch the glasses from his hands. He immediately held them high above her reach, his eyes still fixed on her face.

"Who are you? How did you get here?" he asked, his expression stunned.

Torvi glanced back at the door hoping Helena would emerge and rescue her from the handsome young man staring at her in shock. She considered bolting into the street to escape, but she couldn't leave Helena's precious glasses. She had to think of something and fast.

"If you just give me my glasses, I'll be gone before you can blink," Torvi promised, reaching for the glasses again.

"You are not moving an inch until you tell me who you are," he said firmly.

In that moment, Torvi decided she had to leave the glasses behind. She pretended to see something strange across the road and pointed, diverting his attention. As soon as he looked away, Torvi sprinted in the opposite direction, running as fast as she could.

She glanced back and was relieved to see him standing there, too stunned to chase after her. Just as she was beginning to feel like she had escaped him, he suddenly flew down from the sky above her, eliciting a scream from her.

"You think you can lose me that quick?" he growled, wrapping his strong hand around her wrist.

"Please, don't hurt me," Torvi pleaded, her voice trembling with fear as she met his intense gaze.

"Hurt you? Never," he replied gently, his eyes softening as he looked at her frightened face. "I'm Zac. What's your name?"

"Torvi," she answered, feeling a wave of relief as he released his grip on her.

Her eyes roamed over his figure, taking in his impeccable attire – a long red coat and black leather pants. His coat was unlike anything she had seen before, exuding an air of luxury and distinction. The long sword strapped to his belt marked him as someone important in the city.

She recalled how he had descended before her moments ago, and curiosity sparked within her about his magical abilities. She admired his long dark hair cascading over his shoulders, his tall frame and his broad, inviting smile. Torvi felt a growing curiosity about him and the city, eager to uncover all its secrets.

"How did you get here, Torvi?" he inquired softly, a curious expression on his face.

"I came through a mirror."

"What kind of mirror, and where is it?" Zac asked.

"I'm sorry, but I can't tell you," Torvi replied, avoiding the gazes of passersby.

People stared at them, but their attention seemed more focused on Zac. This confirmed her earlier suspicion that he was someone important in the city. His tall, handsome appearance drew attention, but she sensed there was more to it than just his looks.

"Why can't you tell me?" he asked, moving closer to her until there was no space between them.

"Because I can't trust you, and I don't know what you would do with that information," Torvi said, taking a step back.

"I could have you locked up until I get every piece of information I need," Zac threatened, his hand encircling her wrist again.

Torvi's heart pounded wildly in her chest as he spoke. She scrutinized him, wondering if he was the master Ann and Helena had mentioned. Instantly, she regretted leaving the showroom without Helena. Her face contorted in confusion as she noticed the wide grin on his face. She certainly hadn't been expecting him to be smiling at her if he was the master.

"Don't look so scared, Torvi. I'm just pulling your leg," he muttered, lifting her chin so she could meet his gaze.

"I told you that I would never hurt you, and I don't go back on my word. Here, put your glasses back on and come with me; people are starting to stare too much."

Torvi took the glasses from him, put them on and followed him without saying another word. She found herself believing every word he said. It was odd, considering how scared she had been moments ago, but her heart felt at peace as they walked through the city.

Zac watched Torvi from the corner of his eye as they walked side by side. He marveled at her exceptional beauty, unable to tear his gaze away. The way the soft breeze played with her hair, and the gentleness of her blue eyes when she looked at him, combined with her quick decisiveness, intrigued him greatly. He wanted to know everything about her, but first, he needed her trust.

He had no intention of hurting her. Instead, he longed to protect her from his father's guards, who prowled the city. It struck him as odd that someone from the outside world would appear just as his father was about to begin his magic of possession. A satisfied grin spread across his face as he imagined his father's carefully laid plans tumbling down like a house of cards.

"Where are you taking me?" Torvi inquired, glancing around her as they passed houses, stores, and small outdoor restaurants.

"Somewhere away from prying eyes," Zac answered, his hand resting on his sword as his long strides quickly covered the distance.

"Where is this place, and why is it called the City of Unutilized Magic when everyone here has magic? And why is everything so sparkly and glowing?" Torvi asked breathlessly, struggling to keep up with his pace.

"Whoa! Slow down, okay? You ask too many questions. Are you a reporter or journalist in the real world?" Zac chuckled, his eyes twinkling with amusement as he glanced at her.

"Wait a minute; you know things about the real world!" Torvi exclaimed, stopping in her tracks.

"Of course, everyone who lives here once lived in the real world," he revealed.

"Then how did you all get here? Is this some kind of world for people who lived unfulfilled lives in the real world or something?"

"I wouldn't call it unfulfilled; everyone reborn here never got to use their magical gifts in the real world. This city offers the opportunity to fully utilize those gifts, but it's quite sad that people are forced to sell off their gifts because they are in dire need of money," Zac explained, his eyes turning sad.

"So, every one of you lived normal lives in the real world before being reborn here?" Torvi asked, marveling at Zac's revelation.

"Yes, every one of us," Zac nodded.

"Does that mean that no one dies here? Like you all live forever?"

"Unfortunately, people die here just like in the real world. But it's different and a whole lot more complicated. Now, we better keep moving. I could get us where I want in a couple of minutes, but I don't want to take off with you with everyone around, so we have to walk a bit more," Zac explained, his hand clamping down on Torvi's and nudging her forward.

"You have the gift of flying, don't you?' Torvi asked as they resumed walking. "I noticed how fast you caught me back at the showroom; you were right in front of me before I could blink!"

Zac's heart tightened as he glanced at Torvi's eager face. He loved her curiosity and longed to answer all her questions, no matter how many there were. She intrigued and amused him greatly. There was also something innocent and trusting about her that made him want to take her into his arms and shield her against every hurt or harm in the world.

"Of course, I could fly anywhere I want. We are only walking to avoid too much attention. I wouldn't want anyone seeing me take off with you; it could arouse their curiosity, and that wouldn't be good."

"Who are you, Zac?" Torvi asked, her expression thoughtful. "Everyone looks at you with mixed emotions. I can't tell if they love or hate you because it seems they're struggling with both," she continued.

Zac was taken aback by Torvi's keen observation. He stared at her with renewed interest, marveling at her perception. Just as he was about to respond he noticed Caden approaching, his biceps gleaming in the afternoon sun. Instinctively, Zac tightened his grip on Torvi's wrist and he drew her closer, his other hand resting lightly on his sword.

Torvi's heart skipped a beat as she recognized Caden, the guard she had seen near the oak trees. She looked up at Zac in surprise, noting the sudden change in his demeanor. He had transformed into a fierce warrior, ready to defend at any moment.

"I see you've got company," Caden said with a smirk as he approached.

"It's none of your business," Zac snapped, his eyes blazing with anger. "Now, out of my way," he demanded, attempting to move past Caden, who quickly blocked the way with his imposing frame.

Caden's eyes scanned Torvi, his gaze lingering on her glasses.

"I hope she knows you're getting married soon. We all know your father's orders are final, and you wouldn't want her poor little heart breaking, would you?" Caden said, turning his attention back to Zac.

Torvi's eyes opened wide in shock at Caden's words. Ann's warnings echoed in her mind as she tried to calm her racing heart. She couldn't believe she had been conversing with the master's son, the one destined to marry the Fire Princess.

Suddenly, everything made sense to Torvi. His dignified appearance, the expensive clothes, the sword, and the curious glances from passersby as they walked through the city. She couldn't believe Zac was the son of the master who bought people's powers and ruled the city from his mighty castle. She felt his grip on her wrist tighten, a slight burning sensation beginning to spread.

The atmosphere was tense as Zac and Caden sized each other up, neither making a move but both keeping a wary eye on the other.

Caden's stance was challenging, as if daring Zac to start a fight. Zac took two steps forward and stood face to face with Caden.

Although they were the same height, Caden was heavily built, while Zac was tall with a broad chest and strong arms that showed clearly through his long red coat. Caden's huge frame blocked their view, and Torvi wondered if the two men were about to engage in physical combat. From the look in their eyes, she was certain there was a long-standing animosity between them.

"Need I remind you of your job description, Caden," Zac began hotly, his eyes blazing with fury. "You are just a guard. Your role is to keep the city protected, not to nose into other people's business. Remember your place and your station!"

"I might be just a guard, but your father trusts me more than you, his own son," Caden boasted, a smug smile on his face.

"Trust, huh?" Zac scoffed, shaking his head. "You must think highly of yourself to believe my father trusts anyone. You're just his little puppet, sent on all the dirty errands. He'll soon dump you for the next loyal lap dog that comes along."

"That's not true!" Caden exclaimed, struggling to hide the hurt in his eyes. "I am no ordinary guard to the master; he has great plans for me."

"Keep telling yourself that, maybe it'll help you sleep better at night. But don't say I didn't warn you," Zac chuckled, his voice dripping with mockery.

"You can say all you want; I don't care!" Caden cried out, struggling to hide his frustration. "Master Raul pledged to make me a beneficiary of the magic of possession. You and I both know an ordinary guard wouldn't be privy to such information."

"Well, I'd love to stay and chat about your supposed worth to my father, but I've got more important things to attend to," Zac said sarcastically, staring directly into Caden's face. "Good luck to you and my father with your magic of possession. I'll wait to see how that turns out. Now, out of my way." Zac commanded, his chest colliding with Caden's as he moved past him.

"Just so you know, the magic is important to us, and I don't want you messing it up," Caden called out, watching Zac's retreating back.

"I'm curious to see how successful it'll be in giving you both the immortality you desire," Zac remarked, his gaze fixed ahead.

"At least we would be immortal and not die like your sweet mother," Caden taunted, laughing at his own joke.

Zac stopped in his tracks and whirled around abruptly, dragging Torvi along with him. He let go of her hand and was in front of Caden in a split second, his breath coming out in loud, angry gasps. In one swift move, he grabbed Caden by the neck and flew high up into the sky with him.

"I might not be able to kill you, but I can make your remaining life so miserable that you'll wish for death!" Zac threatened, his voice trembling with rage. "How about I throw you down from up here? A dozen broken bones and legs that no longer work would be just perfect for you right now."

Caden shivered as he looked down, his eyes wide with terror. He clung to Zac's arms, Zac's coat billowing around them in the strong wind. "Please, Zac, don't throw me down," Caden pleaded, his eyes squeezed shut in fear.

"Don't you ever say anything about my mother. Keep her out of your shady deals with my father. The next time you do, I won't hesitate to throw you from the highest peak. Never mention her again, do you understand?" Zac yelled.

"I... underst... please..." Caden stammered, refusing to let go of Zac's arms.

Zac descended and threw Caden to the ground from a short distance, his heart pounding with anger. Without a word, he grabbed Torvi by the arm and began to walk away, pain evident in his eyes. The onlookers stared, but he didn't spare them a glance.

Torvi struggled to keep up with Zac's brisk pace, half walking, half running to avoid being dragged. She knew he was angry and kept silent, understanding how much he loved his mother and how close they had been. The raw pain in his eyes showed he was still reeling from her loss.

As they neared the edge of the city, the houses grew smaller, and the crowd thinned. Torvi remembered Ann's words and scanned the area, hoping to locate her house. Suddenly, Zac stopped so abruptly that Torvi almost bumped into him. She looked up at him in surprise as he gathered her into a tight embrace. Before she could speak, he took off into the sky with her, holding her firmly in his arms.

Torvi's head spun as they ascended. At first, she was too scared to open her eyes, clinging tightly to Zac, loving how his strong arms held her protectively. She could feel the wind in her hair and the sun on her face.

"Torvi, open your eyes," Zac whispered into her ear, his breath hot on her cheek.

"I can't, I'm so scared," she whimpered, clinging tighter.

"Don't worry, I've got you."

"Sure?"

"Sure."

Torvi opened her eyes and looked at Zac. The assurance in his eyes gave her the courage to look down.

"Whoa! It's so beautiful from up here!" she exclaimed, watching the city below.

"Just wait until you see where I'm taking you," Zac chuckled, delighted by her excitement.

Torvi watched in fascination as they left the glittering city behind, flying over lush green grass and trees. The only company they had were the birds who flew alongside them. She smiled happily at the birds, and they seemed to recognize her smile, responding with cheerful chirps.

"Those birds are my friends; they fly with me every day," Zac explained, noticing the astonishment in Torvi's eyes as two of the birds settled on his shoulders.

"Do you fly here every day?" Torvi asked, reaching out to gently touch one of the birds.

"Yes, it's the only way I can clear my head from everything happening in my father's castle. Now, hold on tight; we're about to land."

Torvi held on tightly as they made a quick descent to the ground. In front of her stood a little white cottage, surrounded by blooming flowers. The cottage was nestled among tall trees, providing it with both shade and seclusion.

"Where is this?" Torvi gasped, taking in every detail around her.

"This is my safe haven," Zac replied, still holding her in his arms.

The flowers around the cottage reminded Torvi of her aunt's garden. She disentangled herself from Zac's hold to take a proper look. Walking to a bunch of red roses, she bent down and breathed in their sweet fragrance, her eyes closed in delight. The place was calm, far from the city's noise. Beside the cottage was a narrow path leading into the thick trees, where the soft chirping of birds could be heard.

Torvi began to walk towards the narrow path, eager to explore what lay ahead. After just a few steps, she heard a low growl coming from the trees. A large white bear emerged, moving slowly towards her. She fled back, clutching Zac's arm tightly.

"You don't have to be scared; it's just my friend, White," Zac muttered, taking slow steps towards the bear with Torvi hiding behind him.

"White?" Torvi gasped, peeking at the bear.

"Yes, White has been my friend since he was little. He keeps me company whenever I venture out here."

Torvi watched with wide eyes as Zac knelt beside the bear, stroking its head and body. The bear leaned affectionately towards him, as though in a hug.

"Don't be scared; come say hi,' Zac urged, holding out a hand to Torvi, who hesitated in fear.

"I don't know…"

"Come on, trust me." There was something in Zac's voice – something true and sincere – that made her feel safe. Nodding, Torvi took slow, confident steps towards the bear. The bear looked up at her as she reached out and laid her palm on its warm body. Just like with Zac, the bear leaned towards her, rubbing its head against her legs.

"See? He likes you already," Zac smiled, giving the bear an affectionate squeeze.

"He's so beautiful!" Torvi gushed, feeling at ease with the bear around her.

"Yes," Zac said, standing as the bear retreated into the trees.

"Zac, forgive my curiosity, but I need to know more about this city and its glittering allure. What did Caden mean about immortality earlier? You've only given me fragments, and my curiosity is burning."

"I promise to tell you everything you need to know Torvi. But first, come inside, and then we can talk."

Torvi nodded and followed Zac into the cottage. The small living room was adorned with heart-shaped white cushions on the couch, and a thick white rug. To the right was a shelf filled with books, and the walls were decorated with framed photographs of a beautiful woman with long, dark hair that nearly reached her hips. Torvi instantly recognized the woman as Zac's mother, noting their striking resemblance.

"She's beautiful," Torvi murmured as Zac joined her, his eyes fixed on the picture.

"Yes, she was the most understanding and loving person I've ever known. It's so painful that she couldn't stay with me longer," Zac said, his voice thick with emotion and tears welling in his eyes.

"What happened to her?" Torvi asked gently, shifting her gaze to Zac.

"Come, sit," Zac said, moving to a couch near the wall and settling into it.

Torvi sat beside him and crossed her legs, her eyes fixed on his face. She knew he was relieved to finally share what she longed to hear, but the sadness in his eyes tore at her heart.

"Remember what I told you about everyone here who once lived in the real world?" Zac began, stretching his long legs in front of him.

"Yes, I do," Torvi answered, moving closer to him on the couch.

"The City of Unutilized Magic is a world created for people with magical gifts who were born into the real world but never got to use them. Many of us never knew we had these gifts and lived our lives in ignorance, going through life like ordinary people without ever tapping into our magical powers.

"When a person with such magical powers dies in the real world, they are reborn here and immediately get to use the gifts that were untapped in the real world."

"Are they reborn here as children again?" Torvi asked curiously.

"Of course, we can't just appear here as grown-ups," Zac let out a small chuckle.

"Go on," Torvi urged, eager to know more.

"Once a child is reborn here, they grow up with the knowledge of their magical gifts."

"Is that why you all have glowing eyes and hands?"

"Yes, the glow in our eyes and hands signifies that we are born with magic. We are no longer of the real world but magical beings living in a magical city," Zac explained.

"The sparkle and diamonds all over the city were placed there by the creator of magic to compensate for the darkness every magical person experienced in the real world."

"But the real world isn't dark," Torvi said, looking confused.

Zac smiled gently as he continued, "All of us who lived in ignorance of our magic can be likened to being lost in the darkness. We never had anyone to explain why we felt different. Our gifts remained trapped inside of us, and we existed in the darkness of our true potential.

"At first, the city blossomed, and everyone lived in total harmony. People built houses with shining bricks and diamonds mined in torrents. It was a gift from the creator, and every family received an equal share of these natural treasures.

"However, things changed when the people chose masters to lead them, as is done in the real world. These masters amassed all the city's natural resources for themselves and introduced buying and selling. They minted gold coins with their faces on them, making the coins the medium of exchange.

"The city was meant to be a haven for everyone born with magic, a place to live freely and enjoy the life they couldn't in the real world. But it turned into a world of chaos."

"That's terrible," Torvi muttered, feeling sad for the city that was once filled with freedom and abundance for everyone. "Didn't anyone try to stop them?"

"No," Zac shook his head sadly. "Year after year, things got worse, and the masters trampled over the people. According to the history books, the masters created so much fear in the people that no one dared challenge them. Then, one day, the creator grew angry at the evil committed and took away the gift of immortality."

"Whoa, people here were supposed to live forever?" Torvi gasped, wide-eyed with surprise.

"Yes, they were supposed to live forever in the wonderful city filled with love and light, but that power was taken away from them. The creator struck all the masters dead and established a new rule for the city.

"He gave everyone twice the number of years they lived in the real world. Instead of living forever, everyone's lifespan now depends on how long they lived in the real world. For example, if someone with unutilized magic dies at the age of fifty in the real world, they would live to be a hundred here."

"But isn't that fair enough?" Torvi asked, a thoughtful expression on her face. "I mean, you all get to live twice the number of years you lived in the real world."

"It could have been fair if we all lived to a ripe old age in the real world, but some people died young, like my mother."

"I'm so sorry; I didn't think about it that way," Torvi muttered, wishing she hadn't been too quick to speak.

"It's fine, Torvi. Anyone would have felt the same way."

"How old was she when she died here?"

"Forty. She was twenty when she died in the real world."

Torvi was silent for a while as she stared at the photograph in front of her. She wondered who Zac's mother had been in the real world. Knowing she died so young saddened her, and she wished the creator hadn't taken away the gift of immortality from the people.

She was astonished by everything that had happened so far and all Zac had told her about the city. Different thoughts flew through her mind as she wondered what it would feel like to live in such a glorious city with all the lights and sparkle.

It was hard to believe that a little exploration of her aunt's old house had led her to a city filled with marvelous people and magical powers. It all felt like a dream, except she wasn't sleeping. Suddenly, she remembered what Caden had said about immortality, and turned to face Zac, eager to find out more.

"What about the immortality magic or something Caden spoke about?"

"That's one of the major problems facing the city, Torvi, and I want you to help me stop it," Zac answered firmly, his eyes burning with determination.

Chapter Four

It took Helena a long time to notice Torvi's absence. She had been engrossed in work, serving and cleaning tables, and hadn't realized that someone else now occupied Torvi's table. She looked around worriedly, hoping Torvi was not in any danger.

Despite having spent only a few moments with Torvi, Helena had developed an instant liking for her and wished for her safe return to her real world. Her eyes anxiously watched the door, believing Torvi would walk back in at any moment, but there was no sign of her.

Hanging her cleaning towel around her neck, Helena was about to step out when a voice from the bar called out to her.

"Where are you going? Get us some drinks over here, miss," the man said, waving her over.

Helena hesitated; her eyes fixed on the open door. She glanced at the man briefly before returning to the bar to fill the glasses. She decided to stay until nightfall to see if Torvi would return. If not, Helena would have to go looking for her.

BACK IN THE CASTLE, Caden stood before Raul, his hand gripping the hilt of his sword.

"So, who is this young lady you said you saw Zac with?" Raul inquired, a frown creasing his face.

"I don't know her; she didn't seem to be from this city," Caden replied quickly, his eyes locked on Raul's.

"Not from this city?" Raul scoffed, shaking his head. "How can you be certain of that? Do you know every woman in the city?"

"No, master, I don't."

"Then why would you stand before me, making assumptions you're not sure of?"

"I'm sorry, master," Caden said, bowing his head.

"Dumb, dumb, dumb," Raul muttered under his breath.

Caden pretended not to hear. Zac's words replayed in his mind, and he stared curiously at his master, wondering if he was merely being used to finish the dirty work and then be discarded.

"No, I won't allow myself to be used and thrown away like some piece of garbage," he thought, struggling to keep a straight face as he stared at the throne Raul sat on.

Caden often nursed the ambition of being a master himself. He admired Raul's power and wished for nothing more than to sit on that throne someday, controlling all the wealth and power the city possessed. He had a plan, a careful plan he would execute only when the time was right.

For now, he would wait. If Raul thought he was the only one who could use people and make them feel valuable, he was mistaken. Caden knew how to play the game, making people see him as just a guard, a puppet to his master. He wouldn't wait for Raul to be ready to throw him out. No, he would make sure to strike first. He had one gift: patience.

"Do you have any idea where Zac and the woman went?" Raul asked, rising from his throne to pace the spacious room.

"No, master," Caden replied, shaking his head. "I couldn't keep up with them."

"Listen, I need you to do something for me," Raul said, stepping closer to Caden.

"Anything, master," Caden responded solemnly, his head bowed.

"I need you to find a way to follow Zac wherever he goes. The half-moon will be out in three days, and the magic of possession will take place at midnight. We can't take any chances, Caden, none at all."

"I will do my best, master."

"Good. Remember, this is for all of us. You will get to partake in the gift of immortality," Raul said, his lips close to Caden's ear.

Caden's lips curled into an ominous smile as he nodded.

TORVI STARED AT ZAC, wondering how she could possibly help the city when she was just a stranger in their world, without any magic. Everything about the city intrigued her, and she had never imagined there would be any problems in a place filled with magic. But she was wrong.

"How can I help when I don't have any magical powers like you all?" Torvi voiced her worries to Zac.

"Your lack of magical powers is exactly why you can help. I'll explain everything soon. I've been thinking of the best way to stop my father from buying magic off the people, and it seemed fate sent you to me just when I needed you the most."

Torvi glanced at the glasses beside her, and her mind instantly went back to Helena at the showroom. Helena had told her that she had to sell her magic because she needed the money, and the raw sadness in her eyes had been so deep. If there was a way she could help, she would gladly do it. It would fill her heart with joy to see Helena use her gift of light again.

"But why is your father taking away their magic, and how does he do it?" Torvi asked.

"Two decades ago, a man with the gift of creating things from his imagination made a possession lamp for my father. This lamp can absorb and store magical gifts. All he had to do was place it beside the person he wants to absorb magic from, and they fall into a deep slumber. He's been buying magic from people in desperate need of money, taking advantage of their vulnerability."

"What about the creator? He gave everything freely, and now they have to pay for it. Why doesn't he come down and set things right with the city again, like he did with the other masters?" Torvi inquired; her interest piqued.

"For some reason, the creator hasn't returned to the city since he took away the gift of immortality from the people. According to the historians, he vowed to return one day but only when goodness had returned to the city. From the way things are, I don't know if that day will ever come," Zac explained, a faraway look in his eyes.

"That's so sad, Zac, but I find it amazing that you don't follow in your father's footsteps. If it were someone else, they might have simply taken after their father and become worse than him."

"I could never be like him, Torvi, never."

"I am ready to help, Zac. Tell me how, and I will gladly do it."

"You have such a kind heart," Zac muttered, gently caressing Torvi's arms. "There's a creek down that small path. We could sit in the fresh air and talk. Come with me."

Torvi placed her small hand into Zac's large one and stood up. He held onto her hand as they walked down the small path.

"Tell me about yourself; I'm curious," Zac said as they walked.

"What would you like to know?"

"Everything."

Their hands swung casually between them as Torvi began to talk. She started with her childhood, watching his eyes widen in fascination as she recounted stories of her aunt's big old house and the deep connection she shared with her. As they walked through the tall trees leading to the creek, she shared details about her family, school, and frustrations at work. Talking to him felt natural, and she didn't hold back.

Soon, they reached the creek and sat on a flat stone near the water. Torvi removed her shoes and rolled up her trousers, letting the warm water lap at her bare feet.

"It's so beautiful out here; everything feels fresh and warm," Torvi remarked, a dreamy expression on her face as she gazed at the serene surroundings.

"Yes, it's one of my favorite places, and I've never brought anyone here before," Zac muttered, looking into Torvi's eyes.

"Oh, then why did you bring me?" Torvi asked softly.

"Because you're special, Torvi. I've been in awe of your beauty ever since I saw you at the showroom," Zac confessed passionately. "Not only are you beautiful, but you also have the purest heart, so full of goodness. You make me want to stay here with you, talking and keeping you close. I love answering your numerous questions and watching your beautiful blue eyes light up with excitement when your curiosity is satisfied. The way you smile makes me want to keep you smiling always. Hearing your delightful laughter sends joy through every part of me."

Torvi opened her mouth, but no words came out. She was too overwhelmed by Zac's outpouring of emotions to find the right words. The fact that she found him breathtakingly handsome wasn't helping. She had stolen glances at him all afternoon, mesmerized by his voice, eyes, hair, and everything else.

It had only been a few hours since they met, but the feelings inside her were powerful. She found herself growing closer to him with each passing second. The connection they shared was strong, as if she had known him for a long time, not just a few hours.

She locked eyes with Zac, her heart beating wildly against her chest. She felt an irresistible pull towards him, like a magnetic force she couldn't resist. He made her heart race and took her breath away. It was the most powerful emotion she had ever felt, warming her all over.

Slowly, their heads drew closer until there was no space left between them. Zac's arms went around Torvi's neck, drawing her closer, pressing her soft breasts against his chest. His lips found hers, and he kissed her gently before pulling back to stare into her eyes.

"You've got me charmed with those eyes of yours, Torvi," he whispered, before placing his lips over hers again.

The kiss was deeper, filled with eagerness and unquenched hunger. Torvi responded with the same vigor, her arms wrapping around his neck. She held tightly onto him, her head swirling as he kissed her with a passion she had never experienced before.

His hands found her nipples through her blouse, and he kneaded them gently, causing her to moan into his mouth. Her eyes closed as she basked in the pleasure of his kisses. Torvi held onto Zac's head as his lips went down her neck, dropping airy kisses as he went.

She could feel the desire spreading through her rapidly, soaking every bit of her. "Yes," she gasped as his hands went underneath her clothing, touching her naked flesh.

Hot desire shot through her as he stroked her nipples, his lips still kissing her with so much intensity. The wetness spread through her center, and she could feel the current passing through her as she squeezed her legs together.

When he brought his lips down and took one of her nipples into his mouth, Torvi cried out in pleasure.

She couldn't think straight, everything was happening so fast, and she found herself wanting more, needing him in a way she had never needed anyone before. She could feel his arousal pressed firmly against her thigh, and she marveled at the full thickness of it. Suddenly, Helena's face flashed before her, and she gently took Zac's head away from her body.

"Is something wrong?" he gasped, his breath heavy, eyes smoldering with desire.

"No," Torvi whispered, taking deep, calming breaths. "But I have to get back."

"Get back?" Zac looked shocked. "I understand if you don't want to stay here, Torvi. I can take you back to the oak trees so you can go home."

"No, you've got it all wrong," Torvi said, shaking her head. "I need to go back to the showroom; a friend is waiting for me there."

"A friend?"

"Technically, yes. I've only known her for a short while, but she gave me these glasses to keep my identity hidden. It's the only diamonds left from what her parents gave her, and I wouldn't want her to think I ran off with them. It's almost sunset, and I'm supposed to meet her back at the showroom. She must be very worried by now," Torvi explained.

"Phew, that's so much better," Zac said, relieved. "For a moment there, I thought you wanted to go back home."

"No," Torvi chuckled.

"Do you trust her? I mean your friend."

Torvi thought back to the beautiful young woman whose first instinct was to protect her. She knew, despite the short time they'd known each other, that her instincts were right. She nodded.

"Good, I will take you back, and you can stay with her for the night. I long for nothing more than to have you here with me, but I understand that you need to return."

"Tomorrow, we could come back here, and you can tell me more about how I can help stop your father from taking away the magic gifts from the people," Torvi said.

"Okay," Zac nodded, stepping down from the stone.

He bent down, helped Torvi put her shoes back on, and pulled her to her feet. They stared at each other with eyes filled with passion, and their lips met in another lingering kiss that left them both gasping for breath.

"Torvi," Zac said softly, stroking her cheek.

"Yes?"

"Promise you're going to be okay."

"Of course, I still have my glasses, remember?" Torvi chuckled, holding up the glasses.

"I know. It's just that I don't know what my father could be up to. He might have that obnoxious Caden following me around so I could fulfill his wish," Zac said worriedly.

"He wants you to marry the Fire Princess," Torvi stated, looking up at him.

"I haven't told you that yet, how did you know?" Zac asked in surprise.

"I hear things," Torvi muttered, a mysterious smile playing on her lips.

"Hmm, well I'm not going to marry her. It doesn't matter what people say."

"Good! So shall we go?" Torvi asked, a hint of eagerness in her voice.

"Yes, there's an opening behind the showroom, and I can get you there without anyone noticing. Someone might be watching me, and I don't want to draw attention to you."

"Seems like a good idea to me."

"Okay, just a moment," Zac said, removing a blue heart-shaped necklace that Torvi hadn't noticed before. "Here, take this."

"What's that?" Torvi inquired, staring curiously at the shining blue object.

"This is a location necklace my mom gave to me when I was little," Zac said softly, a wistful look in his eyes as he gazed at it. "It has a magical power inside of it that is connected to this bracelet." He pulled up his coat sleeve to reveal a gleaming bracelet on his wrist.

"Why are you giving it to me?"

"I want you to have it, I'm not sure, but there might be a need for it. All you have to do is touch the middle of it and hold it, and I'll be right there."

Torvi smiled as Zac lifted her hair and hooked the necklace around her neck. It felt wonderful to see how much he cared about her. He adjusted her hair and gazed lovingly into her eyes, making her feel cherished and desired.

"Thank you."

"Don't thank me. I wish you didn't have to go," Zac whispered, drawing her into his arms.

Torvi eagerly nestled into Zac's embrace, resting her head on his strong, broad chest. She could hear his heart beating against her ear and hugged him tighter. The feelings within her were intense, and just like him, she didn't want to be apart. However, she found solace in knowing they would be together again the next day.

"Okay, time to go," Zac whispered, tightening his arms around her.

"Whoa!" Torvi exclaimed as Zac lifted her into the sky with him.

She clung to him, marveling at the beautiful city below. Unlike the first time, when she had been terrified of flying so high, she now laughed with excitement as the wind blew around them, her long blonde hair streaming freely.

"I'm flying! Flying!" she yelped, making Zac chuckle with delight.

The sun had set, and the city was even more stunning by nightfall. Houses gleamed naturally in the dark, while stores, restaurants, and other places shone brightly, creating a breathtaking vista. Torvi's gaze swept across the sparkling cityscape, feeling as though she were in a fairy tale, with a level of dazzle and magnificence no story had ever captured.

True to Zac's words, there was a quiet opening at the back of the showroom. Torvi was grateful that no one was in sight as he gently set her down on the stairs.

"That was the best flight ever!" Torvi laughed, brushing her hair out of her eyes.

"I'm glad you enjoyed it, ma'am. I'd love to take you on another flight soon," Zac said, pretending to tip an invisible hat toward her.

"Of course, I would want nothing more," she said with a smile.

"Are you sure your friend is waiting in there for you?" Zac asked, his tone serious.

"Yes, she is," Torvi replied confidently.

"What's her name?"

"Helena."

"Okay, remember the necklace around your neck?"

"Yes, I remember. Don't worry, Zac. I'll be just fine."

"Alright, meet me back here tomorrow at sunrise," Zac muttered reluctantly.

"Sure, I will," Torvi nodded, her reluctance mirroring his.

"Go ahead, I want to see you get safely inside."

"Okay," Torvi nodded, taking slow steps toward the door.

"Torvi?" Zac called just as she was about to pull open the door.

"Yes?"

"I had one of the best moments of my life today, thank you," Zac said, his eyes meeting hers.

"It was one of my best moments too," she replied, her voice filled with emotion.

"Goodbye."

"Goodbye Zac."

Torvi pushed open the door and stepped inside, scanning the empty corridor leading to the bathroom. She quickly entered, hoping Helena hadn't been waiting for her for long, but the bathroom was empty. She pressed her ear to the door, listening for approaching footsteps, but everywhere was silent.

Her eyes darted as she left the bathroom and walked down the narrow corridor to the showroom. The silence felt strange, considering how noisy the showroom had been that afternoon. She thought she heard footsteps behind her and quickly whirled around, only to realize it was her own footsteps echoing.

Feeling relieved, she walked faster, eager to check on Helena. Her hands hovered near the magic necklace Zac had given her, ready to press it if needed. Her anxiety eased when she peeked through the door and saw Helena cleaning, a mop in her hands. Helena's back was turned, and she hummed softly as she worked, oblivious to Torvi's presence.

"Helena," Torvi called, stepping closer.

Helena jumped, sending the mop flying. She whirled around, relaxing only when she saw Torvi.

"Torvi!" Helena gasped, rushing to hug her tightly. "I've been worried sick about you! Where have you been?"

"I'm sorry for worrying you, Helena. Something unexpected happened," Torvi explained apologetically.

"It's fine, I'm just happy you're all right."

"Let me help you clean up," Torvi offered, picking up the mop from the floor.

"No, Torvi, you shouldn't," Helena disagreed, trying to take the mop from her. "Just sit, I'll be done in a few minutes."

"I want to help, Helena; it's the least I can do."

Helena wanted to argue further, but Torvi had already started cleaning, leaving her no choice but to get another mop.

"So, tell me what kept you away for so long," Helena inquired curiously, glancing at Torvi as she wrung out the mop.

"Okay, promise you won't freak out," Torvi began, resting the mop beside a chair.

"I won't," Helena answered eagerly.

"Are you sure?"

"I'm sure! Come on, Torvi, you're making me more curious." Helena's short curly hair shook as she spoke excitedly.

"Okay."

"Okay? Come on!"

"Helena, I met Zac, and he knows who I am," Torvi blurted out.

"Wait, Zac? You mean Master Raul's son?" Helena asked, the laughter quickly disappearing from her eyes.

"Yes, Helena. He's a wonderful man, and he explained a lot about this mysterious city to me."

"How can he be a wonderful man when his father confiscated most of the city's resources and buys magic from vulnerable people like me who had no other means of getting money?" Helena demanded, her eyes quickly filling with angry tears.

"He's nothing like his father, Helena!"

"How can you be so sure after spending just hours with him?"

"I'm sure. Believe me, he has nothing but good intentions towards the city and everyone in it."

"I can see he has captivated you with his charm and exceptional good looks. He might not support his father, but he's not to be trusted, Torvi. I wouldn't believe a word he said if I were you."

Torvi remained silent for a while, unable to find the right words. She longed to make Helena understand that although Zac and Raul were of the same flesh and blood, their hearts were as different as night and day.

She understood Helena's disdain for Zac. After all, it was his father she had sold her precious magic gift to when she was vulnerable and in need. But she needed Helena to be open-minded and not judge Zac based on his father's actions. She decided to let Helena calm down for a while, remembering Aunt Sonia's advice from when she was little: always let the raging storm pass.

Torvi continued to clean in silence, watching Helena from the corner of her eye. After a while, she saw Helena drop her mop and walk towards her, a remorseful look on her face.

"Torvi, I'm sorry I reacted the way I did," she began, sitting on an empty chair beside her.

"It's fine, Helena. I understand how you feel. I just wish you would give me a chance to explain things to you. Zac isn't anything like his father. If you must know, he is working on a plan to stop his father from carrying out the magic of possession," Torvi explained, sitting down near her.

"You know about the magic of possession?" Helena gasped, her eyes widening in shock.

"Yes," Torvi nodded. "We talked about a lot of things, and even though I don't know the plan yet, I believe it will be successful. Who knows, you might even get your magic back."

"Oh, goodness! I would want nothing more. At least then I could live twice as long as I did in the real world." Helena clasped her hands, hope shining brightly in her eyes.

"Wait a second. What do you mean by that? I thought everyone here gets to live twice the number of years they lived in the real world?" Torvi exclaimed.

Helena's eyes instantly turned sad, and she sighed heavily before looking at Torvi. "One thing I didn't tell you is that once someone sells their magic gift, they lose the second chance. This means I will only get to live for the same number of years I lived in the real world."

"So not only does Raul take away your magic, but he also takes away life too," Torvi muttered, feeling numb from the discovery.

"Yes, it's that bad," Helena said, getting up from the chair to resume her cleaning. "We need to hurry. The keeper of the showroom might be making his rounds soon, and I want us to be out of here before then."

"Okay," Torvi nodded and quickly started cleaning the tables.

"But why would anyone want to sell their magic, knowing how devastating the consequences are?" Torvi wondered aloud as they finished cleaning.

"Most of us had no other choice. I had to do it to save my brother from being locked up by the moneylenders," Helena admitted, taking the mop and towel from Torvi.

"I'm sorry; that must have been tough."

"It was Torvi. I cried for hours afterward. I felt like I had lost everything. Without my magic, there's no reason to stay in the city, but I'm stuck here until it's my time to leave."

"Don't say that, Helena. You're going to get your magic back. I know it," Torvi said with determination.

"I hope so. It would make me feel valuable again. Living without it just makes everything seem empty. It's like living my life in the real world all over again, but it's harder this time because I know I used to have magic like everyone else."

"Don't worry. I'm certain everything will go back to the way was," Torvi reassured, squeezing Helena's hands.

"Thank you. It feels so much better talking to you about it," Helena said, looking at Torvi with gratitude.

"I'm happy to hear that," Torvi replied softly.

"Let's go home; my house is only a few minutes' walk from here."

"Alright."

Torvi helped Helena lock up, and they began to walk through the city.

"So, what about your brother?" Torvi asked, glancing at Helena.

"He's fine," Helena sighed. "But I don't know if he will ever forgive himself."

"Forgive himself for what?"

"For making me sell my magic. He blames himself for getting involved in gambling in the first place, and now he spends most of his days locked up in the house, refusing to do anything else."

"Oh, that's so sad," Torvi commented, feeling pity for the young man she hadn't met.

"I just wish he would stop blaming himself and realize that what's done is done. Wallowing around locked up in his room won't change anything."

"Maybe I can talk to him, who knows, he might listen to me," Torvi said hopefully, already warming up to the idea.

"I would be delighted if that happens. I love him and want him to go back to the person he used to be. Getting out of the house will be the first step to getting himself back, and I can't wait to see that happen," Helena said optimistically.

As they walked, different thoughts occupied Torvi's mind. There were still dozens of questions she needed answered. Her mind wandered back to her aunt's house, and she wondered if it was nightfall there too. So far, she was enjoying everything about the City of Unutilized Magic. Everything was thrilling, and the fact that she could help make a difference in the city made it even more interesting.

Suddenly, she felt like she was being watched. She looked up and saw Caden staring at her from a distance. Torvi's heart thumped wildly against her chest as he began to walk in her direction. Her hand instinctively found its way to the necklace Zac had given her, and she took long, calming breaths, knowing that he would come to her aid immediately if needed.

Chapter Five

Torvi watched Caden intently as he approached, wishing he would take another route. However, he kept coming straight towards her, his gaze fixed on her face. She clutched the necklace tightly, feeling undecided. Although Caden had seen her with Zac earlier, she was sure he hadn't suspected anything about her. He had simply thought she was Zac's lover.

Now, as he approached, there was no way to know if he would just pass by or stop to ask her some questions. Calling Zac over would attract more attention, and she didn't want that. She knew their plan had a higher chance of succeeding if she didn't draw much attention to herself and Zac.

"Torvi, you seem so uneasy. Is it because of Caden?" Helena observed, turning to stare curiously at her.

"Yes, I don't know if he will stop to ask me questions," Torvi muttered, slowing her pace.

"Why would he? You've done nothing wrong, so there's nothing to worry about," Helena reassured her.

"He saw me with Zac earlier, and they got into a heated argument. I just don't know," Torvi replied.

"What do you want us to do?" Helena asked, stopping to stare at Torvi.

"I guess we have to keep going. Turning back now would only increase his curiosity about me."

"Okay Torvi, just keep a straight face and act normal. Don't give him a chance to think you've got anything to hide."

Following Helena's advice, Torvi walked past Caden with her head held high. She didn't flinch when he slowed down in front of her and looked her over. Just as she began to relax, she heard his returning footsteps and gasped, wishing she had pressed the necklace after all.

"Hey, hold on," he called out, hurrying to stand in front of her.

"What do you want?" Helena demanded, protectively holding Torvi's hand.

"I wasn't talking to you. I want to speak with the blonde," he said, nodding towards Torvi.

"Yes? What do you want?" Torvi asked in a firm and courageous voice.

"Are you Zac's lover? I haven't seen him with you before, so you must be new," Caden sneered.

"I don't see how that is any of your business!" Torvi retorted, her heart pounding fast.

"You're not the only one he's been with you know. He might make you feel special, but you're just like the others who got dumped like an old rag," Caden gloated, stepping closer to her.

Torvi felt stung by Caden's words. For a moment, she wondered if he was right. Zac had made her feel special all afternoon, but was it just one of his ploys?

She swallowed and straightened herself, determined not to give Caden the satisfaction he craved. She could tell he was only trying to get to her because of the embarrassment Zac had inflicted on him earlier.

"I don't care what you say, Caden," she declared, taking a step back. "Now, if you'll excuse us, we have more important things to attend to."

Caden quickly grabbed her hand and pulled her forward, his breath heavy. "You can try all you want, but Zac will have to obey the master's orders. Keep living in your delusion until then."

"Let her be!" Helena shouted, stepping towards Caden.

"What will you do if I don't? You've got no magic, and neither does your friend."

"If you don't let go of her this instant, I'll scream and tell everyone you're trying to molest my friend. Not even your beloved master will save you from the angry mob. And you, a guard who's supposed to protect the city, it will only make things worse," Helena threatened with a smirk.

Caden quickly let go of Torvi's hand and stepped back, his eyes scanning the surroundings. People were already throwing curious glances their way, and a group of men were pointing in their direction.

"Remember what I told you. You mean very little to him," he called out as he walked away.

"That was easy," Torvi said, surprised, as she turned to look at Helena.

"Yes," Helena nodded.

"Let's go." Torvi's heartbeat returned to normal as they continued their walk. For a brief moment with Caden, she had feared he might discover her true identity and complicate everything, but Helena had quickly found a way to drive him away.

"Helena," Torvi called after a moment of silence.

"Yes?"

"What he said back there..."

"About what?" Helena inquired.

"What he said about Zac, is it true?" Torvi forced the words out.

"Of course not! Torvi, why would you believe anything he says?"

"No, I don't. I just wanted to know if..."

"If Zac had dozens of other women?" Helena interrupted.

"Yes."

"I will be honest with you, Torvi. You know what I used to think about Zac. Until this evening, I've always thought he was as evil as his father Raul. But despite my initial feelings about him, one thing I'm sure of is that he isn't anything like what Caden said he was."

"Really?" Torvi asked, feeling relieved.

"Yes. Most women threw themselves at him, and I hear them on the streets, complaining about his aloofness and wondering if he was some kind of monk in a past life. I wouldn't worry about it if I were you."

"Phew! That's good to know," Torvi grinned, the worry disappearing from her voice.

"Are you in love with him?" Helena asked softly.

Torvi was silent for a while as she tried to understand her feelings. Spending the afternoon with him had been delightful. When he kissed her, the sensation that spread through her body was instant. She longed to be in his arms again, to be kissed by him, to feel his body against hers. Never had she experienced such a powerful connection with anyone, a feeling that both thrilled and slightly confused her.

"I don't know what it is right now, but there's this special connection between us, and I can't stop thinking about him," Torvi confessed, turning to look at Helena.

"I can see you like him a lot already, Torvi. Maybe you're a little in love?" Helena suggested.

"He's just so amazing, so funny, and oh, so handsome. I can barely look away from his face," Torvi gushed, hugging herself.

"Oh, Torvi, you are in love; you just don't realize it yet," Helena laughed.

"I guess," Torvi chuckled, her mind drifting back to the moment they shared at the cottage. The way his lips cascaded down her neck had left her breathless and wanting more. It took all her willpower to leave his arms. If not for her concern about Helena worrying, she knew their kisses would have led to intense and passionate lovemaking.

There was no doubt in her heart that she wanted him, and she looked forward to the next day with anticipation. She didn't want to think about the future or worry about staying in the city. All she wanted was to go with the flow and allow herself to love and be loved without any restrictions. She felt fortunate to have found such a magnificent place far away from her real world, and she was ready to explore all it had to offer.

If finding love with gorgeous Zac was part of it, she was ready to bask in it and enjoy every moment. Talking to Zac and learning more about the city had been a wonderful experience. She loved the look in his eyes every time he stared at her, and although he hadn't said it, she was almost certain he was falling in love with her too.

She had been scorned by love in the real world; perhaps she was meant to find love and friendship here. She wondered if her aunt knew about the mirrors. There was no way the mirrors could be in those rooms without her aunt's knowledge. Was that why she never allowed her to venture to the rooms upstairs? Was her aunt aware of the different worlds the mirrors could take her to? Could that be the reason she went up into those rooms alone? Did her aunt also explore, or had she purposely left it for her to discover?

"We're home," Helena announced, jerking Torvi away from her musings.

Torvi looked up at the brightly lit, moderate house in front of her, loving its simple yet charming look. It had short steps leading to the large front door, which was slightly ajar.

"Seems it's open," Torvi observed as they approached.

"Yes, I guess he forgot himself again," Helena sighed, shaking her head.

Helena held the door open for Torvi, who walked into the living room. Glad to be indoors, she took off her glasses and looked around. Soon, she heard the shuffling of feet, and a young man with the saddest eyes Torvi had ever seen entered the room. He stared curiously, his eyes lighting up with sudden excitement.

"Torvi, I'd like you to meet my brother, Jason" Helena introduced.

"Hi, Jason," Torvi beamed, extending her hand. But Jason's attention was fixed on her eyes.

"Why does she look so different? Wait a minute, she's from the real world!" he gasped, moving closer to get a better look at her eyes.

"Yes, Jason, she is," Helena replied reluctantly, her eyes glued to the glasses in Torvi's hands, as if wishing she hadn't taken them off.

"You have to keep this a secret, Jason; we can't afford to let anyone know," Helena warned.

"Of course. Why do you think I'd want to tell anyone anyway?" Jason sounded a bit hurt as he turned to gaze at his sister.

"I'm sorry, Jason. I didn't mean to sound so untrusting. It's just that a lot of things depend on her."

"Like what?"

Helena took a deep breath and turned to look at Torvi, her eyes filled with hope.

"If things work out, she could help me get my magic back. That's why it's crucial her real identity remains a secret."

A look Helena hadn't seen in a long time crossed Jason's face as he stared at Torvi.

"If it means getting your magic back, I'll do anything, Helena. Anything at all."

ZAC COULDN'T STOP THINKING about Torvi as he sat on one of the elegant chairs in the castle. Throughout the night, he had to resist the urge to return to the showroom to see her. He knew how important it was for her to meet up with her friend, and he didn't want to interrupt them, especially with Caden possibly watching.

His strong feelings for her had taken him by surprise, developing so quickly. No other woman had stirred such deep emotions within him. All afternoon, he had been captivated by her beauty, her smile, her curious mind, and even her delightful laughter.

When his lips had met hers, he had simply wanted to wrap her in his arms and kiss her until the moon disappeared and the sun took its place. He wanted to make slow, unhurried love to her under the wide skies and clear air, feeling her smooth, warm skin against his and touching the intricate parts of her body until she cried out in pure pleasure.

Everything about her intrigued him completely, and he couldn't get enough of her. Over the years, he had countless opportunities to be with any woman he wanted in the city, but he had been hesitant. Many were beautiful and attractive, but none had moved him, so he chose to remain unattached. Seeing Torvi had changed everything.

In just a few moments with her, he found himself falling deeply for her. It was unlike any feeling he had ever experienced before, and he loved every bit of it. His lips spread into a small smile as he remembered how fascinated she was with everything around her, and how eager she was to know every tiny detail.

He loved how intelligent and observant she was; her ability to notice things impressed him greatly. He wasn't just attracted to her beauty but also to her personality. He was already looking forward to their time together the next day. There were so many things he wanted to tell her and wonderful things they could do together.

Still smiling, Zac got off the chair and bounded up the stairs two at a time. He was nearly at the top when he heard his father call his name. Turning around slowly, he began to descend, stopping on the third step from the bottom.

"Father, you called," Zac said, watching as his father entered the room.

"Yes, where have you been all day?" Raul inquired, a frown creasing his face.

"Do I need your permission to go about my business?" Zac replied, gripping the stair railing.

"I hear you've finally found a lover," Raul said, taking slow steps toward Zac. "What an irony Zac, just days before your wedding."

"I am never marrying that woman. I've told you that a dozen times!" Zac declared, determined to keep his good mood intact.

"Is she that good? Caden says she's tall and pretty, with long blonde hair."

Zac froze, his heartbeat quickening. For a moment, he feared Caden had discovered her true identity and informed his father. But as he studied Raul's expression, he relaxed and allowed a smile to return to his face.

He knew his father too well. If Raul had discovered that someone from the real world could threaten his magical success, he wouldn't be standing there so calmly. Zac hoped it remained that way; their plans had a better chance of succeeding if Raul remained in the dark.

"I have to go, Father," Zac said, turning and slowly climbing the stairs. "I have other things to attend to, and oh, good luck completing your magic without me."

"Funny of you to think I would let my success depend solely on you," Raul called out, a smirk on his face.

"What do you mean?" Zac gasped, whirling around quickly.

"Oh, you thought I would let all my careful plans fall apart because of you? Ha! Ha! Ha! You must be so full of yourself, son. I have arranged for someone else to marry Fiya. The joining of the blood during the half-moon can be done by any other young man with magic. Zac, the Fire Princess is the only indispensable one, because the fire in her blood will ignite all the other magic and enable the possession to begin."

"What? But I thought..." Zac was too stunned to continue. He stared intently at his father, realizing he had been fooled all along.

"Oh yes, Zac, I only wanted you to partake in it as my son, but since you're so foolish as to throw away a chance at immortality, I will simply give that chance to someone else. You appear dazed, son. Don't you have other important things to attend to anymore?" Raul mocked.

Throwing his head back, Raul let out a hoot of laughter that echoed through the castle, his silver hair swirling around him. With immense satisfaction on his face, he walked away, leaving Zac staring after him in shock.

Zac waited until his father was out of sight before letting the smile he had been holding back spread across his face. He couldn't help but laugh as he returned to his room.

"So clever of you, Father, to think you can ever fool me," he chuckled, sitting on his bed.

It felt so good to have deceived his father, a sweet sensation that reached his very soul. He had feigned shock when his father revealed someone else could take his place by marrying Fiya, but Zac had known it was possible all along.

He knew his father was a clever manipulator and had never underestimated him. He knew there was no way Raul would allow the success of everything to rest solely on his shoulders. Anyone could marry the Fire Princess, and the magic would still proceed.

Unknown to his father, Zac also had access to all the books and knew the rules concerning the magic of possession. He would let his father believe everything was going according to plan. It would give him immense satisfaction to see the look on his father's face when he realized that his son had always been a step ahead of him.

TORVI OCCASIONALLY glanced at Jason's face as they sat at the table eating dinner. He looked up at her with hope in his eyes, strengthening her resolve to help in any way she could. She had been deeply touched when Helena told her how guilty Jason had felt ever since she sold her magic to free him from the moneylenders. He seemed so withdrawn, and although Torvi had not yet seen him smile, she was certain it would be just as bright and infectious as Helena's.

"Hope the pasta isn't too bad?" Helena asked, breaking the silence. "I had to whip it up in a rush, so it doesn't taste half as good as it usually does."

"Come on, it tastes just fine, way better than the one I usually make," Torvi chuckled, putting her fork down and taking a sip of water.

"It feels great knowing I didn't totally mess it up." Helena said, stifling a yawn.

"You seem so tired; your eyes are half closed already," Torvi observed, staring at Helena's tired face.

"To be honest, I am exhausted," Helena confessed, her voice low. "I have been on my feet all day, and there was a higher turnout at the showroom today."

"Go get some rest. I will clear the dishes," Torvi offered, already getting up from her chair.

"No Torvi, I will handle it. You are my guest, and you shouldn't be doing the dishes."

"Helena, it's not a big deal, okay? I will finish up in a few minutes and then join you."

"I'll do it," Jason suddenly spoke up, surprising them all. He had been silent throughout their previous discussions, even though they had tried to make him contribute several times. He only sat there, picking at his pasta.

"Are you sure about that?" Helena inquired, looking surprised as she stared at him.

"Yes," he responded simply, nodding his head full of dark brown hair that almost touched his shoulders.

Helena nodded and got up, stifling another yawn. "Alright, I will leave you two then. Goodnight."

"Goodnight," Torvi said softly, noticing Jason's head bowed over the table.

As Helena walked to the bedroom, Torvi glanced at Jason and saw his eyes following Helena's every movement. The regret and sadness in his gaze tore at her heart, making her want to wrap him in a comforting embrace.

Without saying a word, she began stacking the dishes, and Jason joined her. Together, they carried them to the kitchen. Jason washed the dishes, while Torvi rinsed and dried. The only sounds were the gentle clinks of dishes against the sink. When they were finished, Torvi dried her hands and handed the towel to Jason, who took it silently.

"I'm just going to get some fresh air before turning in for the night," she said, giving him a quick glance before stepping out of the kitchen.

The soft air caressed Torvi's skin as she sat on one of the stairs, gazing up at the clear, moonlit sky. The city sparkled before her, and she wondered what the time was in the real world. Was it night-time already, or was the time shift different?

Would her parents try to reach her to confirm she had arrived safely at Aunt Sonia's house? Would they worry if they called her and she didn't answer? Most intriguingly, would they drive over to the house to check on her?

That morning, she had spoken with her mother, who felt that staying alone in the big old house for a month's vacation was a bad idea. She had asked Torvi to come and spend some time with them instead, but Torvi refused.

Although she loved her parents and enjoyed spending time with them in the city, she didn't feel like visiting them at that moment. She knew they would worry about her and try to find out why she was unhappy. The last thing she wanted was to burden her parents with her problems. She was an adult and could handle her difficulties herself. Besides, if she had stayed with them, she wouldn't have found the mirrors and come to this place. She was having the adventure of her life and wouldn't trade it for anything, not even for her mom's delicious pancakes that she loved so much.

The sound of approaching footsteps made her turn around, and she saw Jason standing at the door, looking down at her. He seemed to want to join her on the stairs but appeared unsure. Torvi smiled broadly and waved him over, adjusting her position so he could sit.

Quietly, he sat beside her, and they stared at the sky in silence. She could feel the pain in his unspoken words and understood how hard it must be for him to wake up every day knowing that his sister had given up her magic to save him.

"It's so beautiful out here, Jason," Torvi began, glancing at him from the corner of her eye.

He was silent for so long that Torvi thought he wouldn't respond.

"Nothing seems beautiful anymore," he answered at last, looking up at the sky with sadness in his eyes.

"Why would you say that, Jason? You can't blame yourself forever."

"I feel so guilty. Each time I look at her hands and see the gleam gone while I still have it in mine, I get so consumed with self-loathing that I avoid looking at her caring eyes." He gulped, tears gathering in his eyes.

"Listen, Jason, you made a mistake, but don't we all? Everyone has made a wrong decision at some point in their life, but you don't have to always beat yourself up over it."

"I just can't help it, Torvi. She didn't have to sacrifice so much for me, but she did, and I feel so bad about it."

"I understand perfectly," Torvi said, laying a comforting hand on his arm. "Your sister loves you, and she's so worried about you."

"Really?" Jason questioned, wiping his tears with the back of his hand.

"Yes, she's been bothered by your silence and mood since the incident. You only make her more worried by locking yourself in and refusing to go out or see anyone. She doesn't hold a grudge against you, Jason. All she wants is for her brother, who used to be so full of life, to come back to the way he used to be."

"I didn't know she would feel so worried. I just thought she'd hate me, you know, for everything." Jason sobbed, his voice trembling.

"Helena will never hate you. From the short time I've spent with her, I can tell that she loves you too much to ever think that. Your past mistakes shouldn't define you, and neither should you live the rest of your life in regret, okay?"

"Thanks so much, Torvi. I feel bad that I disappointed her, and she had to pay for it. If there was a way I could pay for my own foolishness, I would have done that a long time ago. It just... it just hurts so much...."

"Come here," Torvi interrupted, extending her arms toward him. She held Jason tightly until his sobs finally became a soft whimper. After a while, he looked at her with a hint of embarrassment.

"Sorry for being so emotional," he said, a small smile forming on his lips.

"Don't worry about it," Torvi chuckled, feeling elated to see the smile on his face.

Torvi stared at the sky above her. "I better get some sleep. I have a long day ahead of me tomorrow," she muttered, stretching her legs.

"I'll stay out here for a little while. It's so peaceful," Jason said softly, turning to gaze at the moon.

"Alright, good night, Jason."

"Goodnight, Torvi."

"Oh Torvi?" Jason called just as she was about to open the door.

"Yes?"

"I am deeply grateful; you don't know how much this means to me."

"I'm glad I could help, Jason," Torvi murmured, feeling moved by the look in his eyes.

She felt light-hearted as she walked through the living room to the bedroom, where Helena lay sound asleep. Sighing in contentment, she slipped under the covers. Her first day in the City of Unutilized Magic had been filled with discoveries and warmth. She couldn't wait to see what events would unfold next.

Chapter Six

Helena woke up to the enticing smell of pancakes drifting in from the kitchen. At first, she assumed Torvi was cooking, but when she turned to the other side of the bed, she saw her still sleeping soundly.

With a puzzled expression, she put on her slippers and slowly walked to the door rubbing her eyes. The aroma grew stronger as she approached the kitchen, prompting her to quicken her pace.

The sight that greeted her left her in stunned silence. Standing at the stove, wearing a white apron and frying pancakes, was Jason. He looked so content and at peace, humming softly to himself. Helena didn't realize she was crying until she felt the tears streaming down her cheeks. She couldn't remember the last time she had seen Jason so happy, singing to himself while he cooked.

He had been quiet and withdrawn for so long that she had almost forgotten how much he loved to sing. The sudden surge of joy that filled her was so overwhelming that she cried out loud, causing Jason to turn toward her.

Jason rushed over to her and they embraced tightly, both sobbing uncontrollably. "I'm so sorry for everything, Helena," Jason sobbed, clinging to his sister. "I never thought…"

"Shush, it's all in the past now," Helena whispered. "I'm just so happy to see you back to being yourself again. It was so hard living with your silence all this time. I missed you so much, Jason."

"I missed you too," Jason whispered.

Torvi stood at the kitchen door, tears in her eyes. Like Helena, she had woken up to the mouthwatering aroma of pancakes. She had hurried to the kitchen, and the scene she encountered melted her heart.

A strange smell drifted through the kitchen, and she frowned. It took her a moment to realize that the pancakes were burning.

"The pancakes!" she exclaimed.

As Helena and Jason rushed to save the pancakes, Torvi threw her head back and laughed, feeling optimistic that everything would turn out just fine.

TORVI WATCHED AS THE city unfolded in the early morning sunlight. A few people were already milling about the streets, each busy with their own goals. She and Helena walked side by side to the showroom, eager to arrive before the crowds.

Torvi still wore Helena's glasses, along with borrowing a pair of deep blue trousers and a white fitted blouse that hugged her breasts and showed off her flat stomach.

As they walked through the city, Torvi couldn't help but marvel at the smiles on everyone's faces. From her observations, she could tell that most of them were cheerful and happy with their lives.

She wasn't surprised at how quickly she was getting attached to the city. In just one day, she had met wonderful friends who made her feel as though she had known them for a very long time.

Everything about the extraordinary city fascinated her. The different people with magic and how they showcased their gifts at the showroom had left her in awe. She found herself wishing she had magic too.

She smiled to herself, imagining what magical gifts she would choose if given the opportunity. Her mind drifted back to the exhilarating moment when she was high up in the sky with Zac. It had been such a thrilling experience that she didn't want it to end. She imagined having that sort of gift in the real world - how awesome it would be to get wherever she wanted in minutes and take people along with her. She was certain she would choose the ability to fly.

Torvi smiled to herself, remembering that she would be meeting Zac shortly, and he would be taking her for another joyful ride in the sky.

"Why are you smiling so much?" Helena asked, turning to stare at her.

"Oh, nothing much," Torvi chuckled. "I'm just looking forward to meeting Zac today."

"I bet you dreamt about him all night," Helena teased, playfully jabbing Torvi's shoulder.

"Well, yes, I couldn't stop thinking about him, even though I was utterly exhausted," Torvi admitted. "Helena? Have you ever been in love?"

"Yes, I have, but it's been over a year now." Helena's eyes looked sad as she turned to Torvi.

"What happened?" Torvi inquired gently. "You don't have to say anything if you don't feel like it," she added quickly when she saw the hesitation in Helena's eyes.

"No, Torvi, why wouldn't I want to tell you? It's just that remembering it makes me feel so sad. His name was Jay, and he was one of the best things that ever happened to me. It was love at first sight, just like you and Zac."

"You speak of him in the past tense. Is he...?" Torvi couldn't finish her words as she watched Helena nod sadly.

"Jay died, and I felt like he took a part of me with him. He died on his fifteenth birthday in the real world, so he lived here for only thirty years. I met him when he had just two years left here."

"That's so sad."

"Yes, but I know I helped make those last two years some of the best he ever had," Helena said softly.

"So, have you ever thought of giving love another chance?" Torvi asked, as they approached the showroom's stairs.

"Not really. I have been too occupied with other things to give it much thought," Helena replied.

"Not to worry, you will find the one for you when the time is right," Torvi said as they walked up the stairs.

Torvi felt her heart beating with anticipation as Helena unlocked the two large double doors to the showroom and pulled them open. While Helena began setting things up, Torvi walked through to the back door, eager to see Zac. It felt as though she hadn't seen him for ages, even though it had only been a few hours.

Pushing open the door, she saw Zac standing with his back to her, staring into space. He wore a long black coat over blue jeans that clung nicely to his legs. High black boots accentuated his tall frame. His long dark hair was left free, and the cool breeze played with the tips, blowing it in different directions.

Her heart pounded as she stared at him. He looked so peaceful and at ease with the world, his hands tucked into the pockets of his coat. Wanting to surprise him, she walked on tiptoes, careful not to let her boots make a sound on the tiled floor.

A wide grin spread across her face as she approached, already anticipating his reaction. Just as she was about to place her hands over his eyes, he spun around suddenly, surprising her instead.

"Zac!" Torvi gasped, laughing as he picked her up and spun her around so fast she had no choice but to cling tightly to him.

"Hey, Torvi, ruined your surprise, didn't I?" he grinned, setting her back on her feet.

"Wait, you knew I was approaching the whole time?"

"Of course, you made so much noise you could wake a sleeping elephant!" Zac laughed, his eyes twinkling with delight.

"Oh, and there I was, thinking I was so quiet." Torvi chuckled, looking up into his eyes.

"I heard the door open and sensed your presence even before I saw you. I decided to let you be for a while."

"Hmmm... Okay."

"I missed you, Torvi. I thought about you all night long," Zac whispered, caressing her cheek.

"I missed you too, Zac, so much."

They stared at each other, eyes filled with love and desire. Zac's lips gently captured Torvi's in a soft, lingering kiss. He cupped her head, and her hands wrapped around his waist, joining their bodies. When they broke apart, they smiled at each other, reflecting their exhilaration at being together again.

"Can you go? I'd like us to leave before the showroom gets crowded," Zac said, his eyes scanning the surroundings.

"I'd love for you to meet Helena before we leave. I've told her a lot about you already," Torvi said happily.

"Great, let's go meet Helena," Zac replied, tucking Torvi's hand into his.

Helena looked up from the glasses she was arranging as she heard footsteps approaching. Her eyes widened in surprise as she saw Zac with Torvi. Quickly, she dried her wet hands on a towel and went over to meet them.

"Zac, this is Helena, my friend," Torvi said, her gaze shifting between them.

"Hi Helena, nice to meet you," Zac said, extending his hand to her.

"Same here, Zac," Helena replied, shaking his hand.

Zac looked down at Helena's hands, noticing the absence of a gleam in them. He stared into her eyes and smiled softly, not wanting to make her uncomfortable.

"Thanks for all you've done for Torvi. You're a wonderful friend, Helena."

"Oh, I should be the one thanking her. She brings so much joy and shares it all around," Helena pointed out.

"Thanks all the same," Zac smiled, letting go of her hand.

Just then, they heard heavy footsteps climbing up the stairs.

"We have to go," Zac said, beginning to lead Torvi away.

"I'll see you back at the house, Helena," Torvi called out, waving as they walked away.

"Alright, be good, okay?" Helena called back.

"I will!"

Torvi and Zac reached the back door just as the front door swung open. They took the back road walking in the same direction as the previous day. Zac held Torvi's hand tightly as they walked.

"Your friend Helena, she sold her magic," Zac said, turning to look at Torvi.

"Yes, she had to do it to save her brother. She had no other choice," Torvi replied.

"That's sad; no one should have to do that. I can't wait for the day when the city's resources are equally distributed, and no one has to sell their magical gifts out of desperation."

"You mentioned your father has a lamp to store the magic he buys. Why does he buy it when he could simply take it from them?" Torvi asked.

"Because he can't just take it. For the magic gift to be transferred, the owner must be willing to sell. My father knows that no one will willingly sell to him unless they are in financial trouble, so he makes sure he controls the city's economy and resources," Zac explained.

"He bides his time, waiting patiently for people who have no other choice but to sell their magic to get what should be available for everyone.

"Day by day, more people find themselves in situations where they have no other options. He's buying more magic every day, and right now, he has enough to start his magic of possession, which will give him the immortality he desires," Zac said sadly.

"How does he plan to do it? How does the magic of immortality work?" Torvi asked.

"I'll explain everything once we get to the cottage," Zac said, wrapping his arms around her. "Shall we? We don't have to walk as far as we did yesterday."

"What about the people around?" Torvi asked, glancing from side to side.

"Don't worry about it. Are you ready?"

"Yes," Torvi nodded, tightening her arms around his waist.

Torvi closed her eyes, surrendering herself to the cool breeze that enveloped her as Zac soared into the sky. After a while, she opened her eyes and locked her gaze on Zac, whose smile broadened as he looked at her.

She glanced around, marveling again at how beautiful the city looked from above. In Zac's arms, she felt relaxed and free, not a trace of fear. Soon, the trees surrounding the cottage came into view.

Letting go of Zac's waist, she spread her arms wide and screamed in delight, shaking her head and letting her hair whip around her face.

"You seem to be enjoying this ride even more than the first time," Zac chuckled, loving her excitement.

"Oh yes!" Torvi gushed, tilting her face to the sky as Zac made a quick descent to the ground.

"And here we are," he said, kissing her forehead.

Hand in hand, they began walking towards the cottage when White appeared from the trees, loping towards them. Laughing, Torvi knelt and opened her arms to embrace the bear.

White leaned into her, and she gently rubbed his fur.

"You've found a favorite quickly, haven't you?" Zac laughed, kneeling beside Torvi and brushing the bear.

"See, even White knows you're wonderful. He'd be happy with just you around," Zac said, watching White stroll back into the trees.

"Maybe he's just excited to have another human here," Torvi replied.

Zac turned Torvi to face him. "I'm not saying this to flatter you, but Torvi, you're one of the most amazing people I've ever known. Your goodness shines from within. I feel lucky to have crossed paths with you."

"You're amazing too, Zac. Seeing how much you care for everyone here makes me adore you even more," Torvi said passionately.

"Thank you," he muttered as his lips crashed down on hers. "I ache for you, Torvi, so much," Zac whispered, rubbing his arousal against her.

"I want you too," Torvi moaned, her head swirling with a whirlwind of emotions.

With one swift move, Zac lifted her into his arms, their lips still locked in a passionate kiss. Torvi held his face in her hands, kissing him fervently as he quickly walked to the front door. Kicking it open, he went straight to the bedroom, and gently laid her on the soft bed.

Slowly, he undressed her. Kissing, touching and caressing every bit of exposed flesh. He unclasped her bra, releasing her lush breasts. She lifted her hips as he pulled her trousers off, leaving her naked before him.

"Your body is so perfect, Torvi," he rasped, covering one of her breasts with his hand. "I want to spend the whole day worshiping every inch of you," he moaned, as his lips found her nipples and suckled on them, one after the other, making her twist on the bed in pleasure.

Torvi sighed in contentment as his lips found hers again, she wanted him with all her heart, and there was no hesitation in her. She closed her eyes and softly whimpered as his lips and tongue slowly explored down her whole body, right to her toes.

"I want to feel your body against mine," Torvi cried out, feeling desperate to touch him.

"I want that too," Zac whispered.

Torvi watched, her eyes filled with desire as he undressed quickly, as though his clothes were on fire. His coat was off in seconds, and he yanked at his shirt buttons, ripping some in the process. She understood exactly how he felt; she was feeling the same way. There was an urgency building inside her with every passing second. She admired his broad chest and flat stomach as he bent to remove his trousers, his handsomeness was undeniable. Her desire for him intensified, and she could feel the wetness between her legs increase in anticipation.

She opened her arms wide and welcomed him back as he moved up the bed to her. While one of his hands rubbed her aroused nipples, he trailed his other hand down to her long slender legs and settled at the entrance of her vagina.

Torvi held tightly to his neck and moaned in pleasure as his fingers found her clitoris, massaging it in a circle. Waves of pleasure shook her as he dipped a finger inside of her and began to thrust quickly.

"Oh yes," she whimpered, closing her legs together and trapping his finger inside of her.

While his hands did delicious things to her body, his tongue was searching her mouth. She sucked on his tongue, moaning as the pleasure inside of her mounted.

"Oh, I'm coming!" she gasped, twisting on the bed as her orgasm began to hit her.

Zac began to move faster; he brought his lips to her nipples while his fingers moved faster inside of her. Soon, Torvi's body began to shudder as her release hit her. She closed her eyes tightly, trembling as the wetness flowed through her, leaving her satisfied and panting heavily.

Opening her eyes, she looked up at Zac, giving him a slow, sexy smile. She could feel his firm arousal pressed to the side of her thigh, and she wanted to feel him deep inside of her. She cupped him, and ran her fingers up the long, thick length of him. He was so hard, and she moaned from the sheer pleasure of holding him in her hand.

"I want you inside of me, Zac, the whole of you," she panted, slowly massaging him as he knelt in front of her.

"I'm dying to be inside you, Torvi. You don't know just how much," Zac whispered, drawing her closer to him. Spreading her legs wider, he began to guide his arousal inside of her, inch by inch.

"Yes, I want more," Torvi gasped, as he stopped halfway through her tightness.

"Oh Torvi, you feel amazing, so warm and tight," Zac whispered, and with one final push, he was completely inside her. Torvi felt herself stretching to accommodate him as he filled every inch of her. They fitted each other perfectly, and she held on to the sheets as he began to slowly thrust inside of her.

"Torvi!" Zac increased the pace, his hands cupping her breasts as he moved.

"Oh yes! Yes! Faster!" Torvi cried out, sensing another sweetness building inside of her.

The sensations he brought out of her body were unexpected, the kind of pleasure that made her want to scream out loud in exhilaration. Lifting her hips from the bed she began to meet his thrusts halfway, letting out loud moans as the sensations grew.

"You drive me crazy, Torvi, so crazy!" Zac gasped, his voice trembling with emotions.

Torvi opened her eyes and stared deep into Zac's. She could see the love and desire reflected in his gaze. The connection between them was fierce, and she couldn't tear her gaze away as another orgasm began to build from deep inside of her.

"I'm coming again!" she gasped, unable to keep her eyes open as the intense pleasure overwhelmed her.

"I'm coming with you. I'm right there with you, Torvi!" Zac moaned, thrusting so hard and fast that the bed began to shake.

The release building inside Torvi was stronger than the first one, and her hands gripped Zac's shoulders as she began to shudder. She heard him groan in pleasure as he slammed harder into her, as though in a frenzy.

It was hot, sweet and consuming all at once. As she neared her release, Zac let out a loud final moan and collapsed against her, shielding his fall with his hands so all his weight would not be directly upon her. She whimpered softly in pleasure as he shot loads of hot cum inside of her.

The euphoria that surged through Torvi was the most satisfying she had ever felt. She cradled his head against her bosom as he shuddered, filling her until the wetness flowed in between them. She felt the rhythm of his heartbeat, perfectly in sync with her own. To her, their union was more than physical; it was a melding of souls.

Zac took long, calming breaths, inhaling the clear, sweet scent of Torvi's skin. He looked up, his gaze lingering on her beautiful face, his love for her filling him completely. In that moment, he resolved never to hold back. She was his, and he wanted to lay bare his feelings, exposing all his vulnerabilities to her.

"Torvi," he called softly, turning onto his back so her head rested on his chest.

"Yes?" she whispered, smiling at him.

Zac felt his heart might burst with all the love he had for her. She was the woman he had been waiting for, and now that she was here, it felt surreal, as though he might wake up and discover it was all a dream.

"I love you so much, Torvi. You are everything I've ever wanted, a dream come true. I am deeply in love with every part of you," Zac confessed passionately.

"I love you too, Zac," Torvi gushed, staring into his eyes. "It didn't take me long to realize that my heart beats for you. It fills me with so much joy, knowing how deeply we feel for each other."

"Oh, Torvi, you don't know just how happy this makes me," Zac said, his eyes glistening with tears as he kissed her forehead. He pulled her closer and stroked her body, from her back down to her bare butt. It felt incredible to know she felt the same way for him. It created a deep happiness inside of him that spread through his whole body.

Zac remained in that position with Torvi in his arms, wishing he could stay like that forever without a worry in the world. But he knew it was impossible. His father was gearing up his plans, and as much as he wanted to forget everything and remain content holding her, he couldn't let his father succeed. There was a lot of planning that needed to be done if he truly wanted to stop him.

"Torvi," he murmured, stroking her long, silky hair.

"Mmhmm," Torvi sighed, feeling utterly relaxed.

"I hate to leave your arms, but we have a lot of planning to do."

"Yes, we need to stop your father. It's more important," Torvi agreed. She started to move away from his arms, but Zac quickly pulled her back.

"Not so fast, darling. How about a quick bath in the creek? Then we can talk with the fresh air blowing all around us."

"Sounds good," Torvi said, rolling off the bed.

She was about to walk to the door when Zac bent down and scooped her up onto his shoulder as if she weighed no more than a feather.

"Zac!" she gasped, laughing loudly as he broke into a small jog with her on his shoulders.

"There you go, miss," Zac chuckled, gently placing her on her feet as they reached the creek.

Holding onto her hands, he led her deeper into the cool water, where they washed off and let the water cascade over their skin. Zac found a large flat rock and placed Torvi on it while he sat on a lower one, resting her feet on his lap.

"It's so beautiful and peaceful out here," Torvi mused, taking in the nature all around them.

"Yes, it is," Zac agreed.

"So, tell me about your plans. How does your father intend to perform his magic of possession?"

"He plans to commence once the half-moon rises tomorrow night. The magic involves several spells which he is going to read from an ancient book he has had for years. Unbeknownst to him, I have a copy of the book in my cottage, so I know all the steps involved. According to the book, anyone who sold their magical gifts loses the second chance the creator granted to all magical people," Zac explained, pausing to see if she understood.

"So, your father accumulates these extra years for himself, gaining immortality!" Torvi muttered, realizing Raul's intentions.

"Yes, exactly." Zac beamed, impressed by how quickly she pieced it together. "Instead of living twice their original lifespan, those years are taken away from them along with their magic."

"When he casts the spells, he will place the lamp at the position of the half-moon. Then, there will be a sacred joining between two powerful magic users. They will stand around the lamp, and the spell caster will slice their palms, ensuring their mingled blood falls directly on the lamp. Once it illuminates, all the magic stored in the lamp will begin to flow out in the form of smoke."

"How does it get transferred to the person?" Torvi asked, her eyes wide in shock.

"Anyone who stands in front of the lamp and inhales the smoke will absorb the extra years the original possessors were supposed to live and their magic," Zac explained, his hands gently caressing Torvi's feet.

"So that's why he wants to join you in marriage with the fire princess. But what happens if you refuse?" she asked, looking confused.

"Torvi, everything will still work perfectly. My father tried to make it seem otherwise, but it was all a fallacy. All he needs is the fire princess and any other young man with magic. I'm sure Caden will be more than willing."

"But Zac, how do we intend to stop him if he can simply proceed with the magic with or without you?"

"I have it all carefully planned," Zac said, a satisfied smile spreading across his face as he looked up at her.

"Oh, please tell me!" Torvi gushed, eagerness burning in her blue eyes.

"The lamp containing all the magic he acquired is protected by a powerful spell. Anyone who comes within five meters of it will be frozen. He has hidden it away in his chambers, and I have no idea where it is."

"So?" Torvi looked puzzled as she noticed the smile spreading across Zac's face.

"So, we wait for him to bring it out and begin his spells."

"And?" Torvi still couldn't grasp the meaning behind Zac's smile.

"Torvi, according to the books, only someone from the outside world can break through the freezing spell protecting the lamp and access it."

Torvi's smiled back at Zac, finally understanding the meaning behind his smile. She flung her arms around his neck, and he kissed her softly, his arousal finding its way into her wetness once again.

Chapter Seven

"Fiya, I believe you are ready for tomorrow night?" Raul asked, a small smile on his face as he sat on his throne and fixed his gaze on Fiya, the fire princess.

"Yes, master. It would be an honor to take part in your magic of possession." Fiya responded, bowing deeply.

She was seated on a chair across from Raul, her glowing eyes occasionally drifting away from his face to admire the impressive walls and designs of the castle. Half of her long white hair was tied up in a bun on top of her head, with the rest cascading down her back, almost touching her hips.

"Good, I am absolutely thrilled to know that you understand what an honor this is," Raul stated with a satisfied smile.

"I know master, but just a question, please."

"Yes?"

"I don't see Zac here. Shouldn't he be around to spend time with me before the wedding?" Fiya asked, looking around as though expecting Zac to appear at any moment.

"Well, there's a little problem, Fiya," Raul sighed, pretending to be disturbed.

"What's that, master?"

"You won't be getting married to Zac tomorrow."

"I am not?" she gasped, her eyes widening in surprise.

"No, but not to worry, I've got the perfect suitor for you."

"But I've always wanted... I thought Zac was...."

"Do you not want the gift of immortality anymore if Zac is out of the picture?" Raul demanded, interrupting her.

"Of course I do. I want nothing more than the ability to live forever," she replied firmly.

"Perfect, Fiya, exactly what I wanted to hear," Raul beamed.

Standing up from his chair, he walked over to her and gently caressed her cheek.

"You are so beautiful, Fiya. It's quite disheartening that you have to be joined with someone else, but who knows? I can do something about it once everything settles down."

"What do you mean?" Fiya asked, meeting his gaze briefly before looking away.

"How would you like to be my Queen, Fiya," Raul whispered, bending a little so that he spoke directly into her ear. "Think about it. Imagine you sitting beside me as my Queen, and together, we will rule this city. No death, just rule forever!"

Fiya's eyes widened in amazement as Raul spoke. She looked up at him and nodded eagerly, her smile growing with each passing second.

"It will be a dream come true, master. I've always wanted to be queen."

"Good Fiya. All this will be possible only if you follow my instructions. Is that clear?"

"Yes, master. I will do exactly as you say."

"That's the perfect answer I long to hear. As for your marriage rites tomorrow, you must remain here at the castle and not be seen until the half-moon rises tomorrow night."

"But master, what about my dress and all the things I've prepared for the wedding?" Fiya asked, her voice tinged with worry. "And my friends, my family, everyone I've told about the wedding?"

"Fiya, you must understand this is no ordinary wedding," Raul said, perching on the arm of her chair.

"I don't understand. Shouldn't my people be there to witness it?"

"No, you can't have anyone there."

"No one at all? But..."

"No buts, Fiya," Raul said firmly. "You will understand by tomorrow. For now, I will call the maids to make your stay here comfortable."

Raul rose and strode back to his throne, pressing the bell beside it. Almost immediately, two maids dressed in black uniforms with aprons tied around their necks appeared, their heads bowed as they stood before him.

"I want you to take Miss Fiya here to one of our special guestrooms and ensure she has everything she needs," Raul instructed, glancing from one maid to the other.

"Yes, sire," they responded in unison.

"Come Fiya, go with them," he motioned to Fiya, who hesitated slightly.

"Okay, master," Fiya nodded, rising to her feet.

"Remember what I told you," he called out after her with a smug expression.

As Fiya departed with the maids, Raul drummed his fingers on the edge of the throne in excitement. Everything he had ever wanted was falling into place. His years of meticulous planning and strategizing were finally paying off, and he couldn't wait. He stared ahead, smiling with satisfaction.

"Immortality, I just can't wait to finally meet you," he murmured, a dreamlike expression on his face.

"YOU'RE A GENIUS, ZAC. I can't begin to imagine how you came up with such an incredible plan," Torvi gushed, her eyes shining with pride as she gazed up at Zac.

They had returned to the bedroom after another refreshing swim at the creek. Zac had his legs and arms tightly wrapped around Torvi, and she relaxed on his chest, loving how delicious it felt to be curled up naked in his arms.

"You flatter me, Torvi. Anyone could have thought of that," Zac chuckled, but he looked flushed with pride as he kissed the top of her head.

"It's true, Zac. Your father is very clever, and it takes someone even more brilliant to outsmart him."

"Yeah, but the odds were in my favor. Despite my meticulous planning, all of it would have been for nothing if you hadn't shown up, Torvi. Everything is falling into place because of you, and I couldn't be more thrilled!" he exclaimed, rolling with her on the bed until he was on top.

"I am beyond thrilled. My friend Helena is going to get her magic back, and the thought of it fills me with so much joy," Torvi said.

"I'm happy about that too, but to ensure our success, we need to make more plans. Does Helena have a brother or sister?" Zac asked, a thoughtful expression on his face as he gazed down at Torvi.

"Yes, she does. His name is Jason. Why do you ask?"

"I'll need someone to create a distraction tomorrow."

"What kind of distraction?" Torvi inquired.

"My father is relaxed right now because he thinks there's no one who can thwart his plans, but knowing him, I'm sure he'll be surrounded by guards because he wouldn't want to take any chances."

"Okay, so how does Helena's brother fit into this?" Torvi asked.

"Er... I'm still figuring that out. Do you know what his magical gift is?" Zac replied.

"No," Torvi said, shaking her head. "I never got the chance to ask Jason, but I will once I get back home."

"Good. I will need both Helena and her brother for the plan I have in mind. When you get home, tell them I want to meet early tomorrow morning," Zac said, smiling as his plans became clearer.

"You've got that mysterious smile on your face again. What's on your mind, Mister Big-time Genius?" Torvi teased, tickling his nose.

"My brain seems to work faster when I'm with you, Torvi. Looking at you gives me the perfect strategy. But first things first, I need to know what Jason's powers are. This will make everything clearer."

"Okay, I will ask Helena. I should go now; she'll be closing the showroom soon, and I want to help her clean up so we can get home in time," Torvi said, trying to get up from the bed. But Zac held her in place, refusing to let her go.

"I know you have to go, but it breaks my heart to see you leave," he murmured, pouting his lips.

"Awww, don't you look cute with those lips of yours?" Torvi teased, kissing him softly.

"Mmm, if you're trying to flatter me, it's working," he whispered, drawing her in for another kiss.

Soon, his kisses became intense, and Torvi could feel his hard arousal against her legs.

"I can't deny what you do to me, Torvi," he gasped, grinding his body slowly against her as he twisted one of her nipples and sucked on the other.

"Oh yes," Torvi moaned, feeling her body responding eagerly to him.

She placed her hands around his neck as he kissed his way down her belly. His touches set her body on fire, and she wanted to reciprocate, to give him half the pleasure he had given to her.

"Zac," she rasped, pulling his head off her body.

"Yes?" he replied, his breathing heavy as he stared down at her.

"I want... I want to be on top of you," she murmured.

Quickly, she turned around and straddled him, her hands softly stroking his chest and arms. Leaning forward she flicked her tongue over his nipples, making him inhale sharply.

While her lips sucked his nipples, her hand trailed down to his thighs, and she cupped his arousal into her palm, massaging it gently.

She grinned as she saw him squirming on the bed, his hands grasping the sheets. Slowly, she kissed her way down his stomach and thighs, before finally taking him into her mouth.

"Torvi!" Zac shuddered with pleasure, his breathing heavy, as he opened his eyes to see her bent over him. "Wha.... what are you doing to me..."

Torvi didn't answer but only increased her movements, her mouth going up and down his sex in quick succession, making him whimper and twist on the bed. She moaned out loud just from the sheer pleasure of having him in her mouth, and hearing the sounds he was making only intensified how ready she was for him.

Unable to hold on anymore, she gently guided him inside her, her eyes closing in pleasure. "Yes," she moaned as she began to move, supporting herself on the bed.

"Oh yes, oh yes," Zac let out, reaching out to grab her waist.

Torvi began to move faster, her hair falling in all directions as she went up and down on him. It felt amazing, knowing that she was bringing him as much pleasure as she was receiving herself.

"Yes, yes, yes!" she cried out in the heat of passion as the sweet sensation began to build deep inside of her, spreading through her body. She could tell he was also near his release, their eyes exchanging the messages their mouths couldn't say at that moment. Their moans filled the air as she rode him faster and faster until they both reached their peaks, then she crumpled into his arms, exhausted but intensely satisfied.

TORVI'S FACE GLOWED in the evening sunset as she adjusted her glasses and climbed the stairs to the showroom. Inside, only a handful of people remained. Helena was busy pouring drinks and picking up glasses. Her face lit up with a smile as soon as she saw Torvi, and she gave her a wave.

Torvi waved back, found an empty chair, and sat down. She was still basking in the euphoria of her lovemaking with Zac, feeling the sensation washing over her as she sat. She fixed her gaze on the stage, where a young man was transforming into different animals, eliciting shouts of excitement from the few spectators around.

Suddenly, Torvi felt as though she was being watched. She glanced around but saw that everyone seemed to have their attention fixed on the stage. She thought she saw a lady in a baseball cap glance her way, but she wasn't sure. Shrugging it off, she focused her attention back on the stage, hoping the crowd would leave soon so she could help Helena clean up and they could go home.

Crossing her legs, she tapped the table with her index finger, nodding along to the music. A burly man with a long mustache approached her, holding a drink in his hand. Just as he was about to pass by, he tripped on the table leg, sending his drink flying.

Before Torvi could move away, the drink landed on her thighs, spilling all over her top and jeans. Helena was by her side in a split second, a towel in her hands.

"Are you okay?" she asked, glancing over Torvi as she squatted to pick up the broken pieces of glass.

"Yes, I'm fine," Torvi nodded.

"Are you sure, Torvi?"

"Yes, Helena, don't worry about it. None of the broken glass touched me. It just landed on my thigh before falling to the floor."

"Hey miss, I'm sorry, okay? Did the glass hurt you?" the man asked after managing to get himself off the floor.

"It's fine. I'm okay," Torvi said politely, noticing that the man was a little drunk.

"Do you... Perhaps I can pay for the outfit I ruined?" he asked, walking a bit unsteadily towards her and reaching into his pocket.

"No, no," she shook her head vigorously. "I'll just go to the restroom and see if I can get some of the stain off the blouse," she said, turning to Helena, who was still beside her.

"Don't be long, okay? I can't wait for them all to leave so I can get off my feet for a moment," Helena muttered with a tired sigh.

"I'll be right back."

Torvi fingered the stain on her white blouse as she walked to the restroom. Pushing the door open, she immediately went to the sink and turned on the tap. She took her glasses off, placed them beside the sink, and stared at her blue eyes in the mirror. The red stain was quite large, so she rolled up her blouse and leaned into the sink, allowing the water to wash over the stained part.

Thoughts of Zac came to her mind, and she smiled softly, eager to tell Helena about the plan he had in mind and how they had to meet early the next day. Abruptly, the door flew open. Without a second thought, Torvi turned, her blue eyes meeting Ann's glowing red ones.

"Ann! It's so great to see you again!" she exclaimed, so happy to see her that she forgot she wasn't wearing her glasses.

"I knew it!" Ann gasped, towering over Torvi. "I knew there was something strange about you when I saw you standing in front of Master Raul's castle!"

"Oh, yes... I..." Torvi stammered, lost for words as she stared at Ann. There was something unsettling in Ann's eyes that made her uncomfortable, the way she scrutinized her with such satisfaction, like a hunter watching its prey.

"Goodness! You're from the real world. My master will be so pleased; he might even grant me the gift of immortality!" Ann declared, clapping her hands excitedly.

"Wait. Your master?" Torvi inquired, her heart pounding as she started to piece things together.

"Yes, Torvi, my master. I am an undercover spy, whose mission is to be the eyes and ears of Master Raul in the city."

"What? So... you acted all friendly with me just to gather information?" Torvi was stunned, recalling how Ann had been so nice to her.

"Yes, at first, I didn't think much of you. But after seeing you with Zac and noticing those glasses, I knew there was more to you. I followed you here, and boom! Here it is. I will go tell him right away, and rest assured, there's nowhere you can hide that the master doesn't know about." Ann beamed, thrilled with her discovery.

"But why are you doing this? I mean, I thought you hated Raul," Torvi asked, trying to keep Ann talking. Her mind raced as she considered her options. She had the necklace Zac had given her, but she knew there was no way he could get there in time. If Ann left the showroom, all their plans would be ruined, and she couldn't afford to let that happen. The happiness of her friend and hundreds of others depended on it.

"Of course I hate Raul, but I have to do what I need to make my life here easier," Ann replied, rolling her eyes.

"So, you're helping him with his evil agenda?" Torvi asked.

"I don't care, Torvi. He pays me well, and that's all that matters," Ann shrugged, moving towards the door.

"I'm sorry, Ann, but I can't let you tell Raul who I am," Torvi said, rushing to the door and leaning against it to block her.

"Out of my way Torvi," Ann said firmly.

"I won't let you do this; you can't tell Raul!" Torvi said vehemently glancing around.

"Okay, just remember I asked nicely," Ann said, charging at Torvi with force.

Torvi didn't have enough time to think; she acted on impulse. As Ann charged with her fist ready to strike, Torvi ducked just in time, causing Ann to collide with the door. Before Ann could recover, Torvi grabbed her by the shoulders and slammed her head hard against the door. Ann immediately went limp and fell to the floor with a thud.

"Oh no," Torvi gasped, kneeling beside Ann to check her pulse. "Thank goodness, she's breathing," she sighed, sinking to the ground beside her and burying her face in her hands.

A couple of seconds passed before she lifted her head glancing around in confusion. "What do I do? What do I do?" she muttered. Suddenly, a knock sounded at the door. She jumped to her feet, panic surging as she wondered where she could hide Ann.

"Torvi, are you in there? You've been a while, so I came to check on you," Helena's voice called from behind the door.

"Yes," she gasped, flinging the door open immediately. "Helena," she cried out in relief, wrapping her arms around her friend.

"Oh my!" Helena gasped, her eyes widening at the sight of Ann's lifeless body on the floor. "What happened, Torvi?"

"I...she..." Torvi stammered; her throat suddenly dry.

"Torvi, calm down, okay?" Helena said, placing her hands on Torvi's shoulders. "Take a deep breath, slowly."

"Okay, okay," Torvi nodded, inhaling deeply. "She knows who I am, and I had to stop her from telling Raul," she blurted out in one breath.

"But who is she?" Helena asked, her gaze fixed on Ann's body sprawled on the floor.

"Her name is Ann, and she's one of Master Raul's spies."

"Spies?" Helena gasped, her hand flying to her mouth in shock.

"Yes. I met her when I first arrived in the city, but I had no idea she had been following me all this time. She came in here when I had my glasses off and discovered who I am. What are we going to do, Helena?"

"We tie her up," Helena replied without hesitation. She knelt and began to loosen Ann's shoelace.

"What? Tie her up?"

"Yeah, Torvi, we have to tie her up until we can figure out what to do next. Do you have a better idea?" she asked, looking up at her.

Torvi thought for a moment and shook her head. She wanted to call Zac, but she could see the wisdom in Helena's suggestion. It was best to tie Ann up so she wouldn't escape. Bending down beside Helena, she began to untie the other shoelace. In no time, they were done, and Helena secured Ann's legs with the rope. The knot was so tight that Torvi worried it might hurt her.

"Let me have that," Helena said, pointing to the other shoelace in Torvi's hand.

"Here, take it." Torvi handed her the shoelace.

Helena repeated the same process with Ann's hands, ensuring she was securely tied. Ann stirred a little, and Torvi rushed to her side, thinking she was waking up. However, Ann soon fell silent again.

"I think she's starting to regain consciousness," Torvi gasped.

"Yes, and that's a problem," Helena sighed. "We don't want her screaming the place down."

"Are there still people in the showroom?" Torvi asked.

"Yes, there are few people left, and I don't want anyone to notice my absence."

"Let's gag her. Once everyone is gone, we can decide what to do with her. But one thing is certain: I won't let her tell Raul everything she knows." Torvi's face was set with resolve as she spoke, surprising Helena.

"Oh great!" Helena beamed. "I like your determination, and I support you. We can't let her ruin everything."

"So, what are we going to gag her with? I don't see anything we can use around here," Torvi said, scanning the restroom for something useful but finding nothing.

Helena also looked around and noticed Ann's open black shoes. She saw a pair of black socks peeking out and immediately had an idea.

"We'll use her socks," Helena decided. She knelt and began to remove Ann's right shoe.

Torvi quickly joined in, pulling off the other shoe. Once the socks were off, she handed them to Helena, who tied them together and used them to gag Ann's mouth.

"Done," Helena panted, as she stood up.

"What if someone comes and finds her here? We'll be in serious trouble," Torvi worried aloud.

"You're right. I was just thinking about the same thing," Helena agreed. She reached into her pocket and handed a bunch of keys to Torvi.

"Here, wait a few minutes after I leave, then lock the door to this restroom. Thankfully, there are other ones available, and the few people around might not need to use this one. We'll figure out what to do with her when everybody is gone."

"Okay, see you soon," Torvi nodded.

"Act calm, okay?" Helena advised, her hand on the doorknob. "I just hope she isn't with anyone who will notice her absence."

"I hope so, too," Torvi sighed.

The two minutes after Helena left felt like an eternity to Torvi. She paced the length of the restroom, occasionally glancing at Ann on the floor. When she heard footsteps approaching, she froze, fearing someone was entering the restroom, but the footsteps moved away.

Torvi placed a hand on her heart, feeling relieved. Zac had told her how clever his father was, but she never imagined he could have spies all over the city. She could only hope that Ann was the only spy in the showroom. If there was someone else with her, Ann's absence would surely be noticed.

Torvi leaned against the door and listened. The silence convinced her it was time to go. Taking one last look at Ann, she opened the door and was about to step out when she remembered her glasses were still beside the sink. She quickly grabbed them and exited the restroom, locking the door behind her.

"Phew! I guess I'm done here for now," she muttered to herself.

She took another look down the corridor, tucking the keys into her back pocket, and tried to act normal as she walked back to the showroom. By the time she arrived, everyone else had left, except for the man who had poured his drink on her. Torvi paused, her eyes meeting Helena's, who motioned for her to sit down.

As soon as Torvi sat, the man stood and began to walk towards her. Helena grabbed a half-filled whiskey bottle and followed closely, hiding the bottle behind her.

Torvi braced herself, certain that the man was working with Ann and that everything had been a setup from the start.

"Hey, miss," he called, his words slightly slurred as he stood in front of her table.

"Yes?" Torvi muttered, her eyes drifting to Helena.

"Did you manage to get the stain off? I just want to apologize for my clumsiness once again," he said, staring at the round stain on her blouse.

Torvi was so shocked by his apology that she was momentarily lost for words. She hadn't expected it, but she decided to remain alert in case it was a ploy.

"Oh, don't worry about it. I've gotten most of the stain off, and I'll be going home soon anyway," she replied.

"Good. I was only waiting for you before leaving. Have a nice evening, miss," the man smiled and turned to leave.

Helena quickly moved away from him, pretending to inspect a table beside Torvi as the man walked away. They watched him closely as he took slow, almost staggering steps to the door. Both released the breath they didn't know they were holding when he exited.

"Torvi, what are we going to do?" Helena asked, slumping into the chair beside her.

"I don't know, Helena, I just don't know."

"We can't possibly leave her there."

"Of course not. Zac said the half-moon will be out by midnight tomorrow, and that's when Raul will begin his spells for the magic of possession. We can't afford to let her out before then, or our plan will be ruined!" Torvi said, clearly distressed.

"Maybe you should call Zac. He'll know exactly what to do," Helena suggested.

"No, we can't call him," Torvi shook her head.

"But why, Torvi? He's our only option right now."

"I believe Raul has people watching Zac. For all we know, there might be lots of other spies out there, and that burly man could be one of them. Making Zac come here will only increase their suspicion. We'll have to think of something on our own."

"So, do you have any ideas right now? She might be awake as we speak," Helena sighed.

Torvi buried her face in her hands, trying to think of ways to keep Ann tied up until their plans were executed, but nothing came to mind. The sound of approaching footsteps made her raise her head immediately, and she tapped Helena, who also looked alarmed. Helena picked up the bottle of whiskey she had dropped and stood up; her eyes locked on the door.

"It's just me!" Jason called out as he stepped into the showroom, a wide grin on his face.

"Jason!" Helena exclaimed, walking up to him with the bottle still in her hands. "What are you doing here?"

"You both were running late, so I decided to come check on you, maybe help you clean or something," he said, glancing between them. "Wait a minute, why do you both look so tense? Is something wrong?"

"Yes, Jason, something happened, and we don't know how to handle it," Torvi replied.

"What happened? Did you guys kill someone?" he joked, a curious expression on his face.

"Something like that," Helena answered, sitting back in her chair.

"Wait, what?" Jason's eyes widened in shock as he stared at them.

Quickly Torvi explained everything to Jason, not withholding any details.

"I think I might have a solution," Jason muttered when Torvi finished talking.

"What solution?" Torvi and Helena asked in unison.

"I know a drink mixture that can make her drunk instantly," Jason began.

"So, how do we give her this drink, and where can we take her?" Helena inquired.

"I'm sure she's awake already. You can simply act caring, you know, just say you want to make her a proposition, but first, you want to give her a drink to quench her thirst. What do you think?" Jason suggested.

"Seems like a great idea," Torvi nodded in agreement.

"Great! Once you get her drunk, we can easily lead her home through the city. If anyone sees two women and a young man supporting a drunk lady, they won't think much of it. These things happen often, so no one will make a big deal out of it. Once we get her home, we can feed her and keep her tied up until everything is done."

"This is perfect!" Torvi declared, jumping up from her chair. "Come on Jason, mix the drink already!"

"Yes Jason, mix the drink and let's hope she takes it," Helena said, leading the way to the bar.

"Oh, I will make her take it. Even if it means shoving it down her throat," Torvi declared, her blue eyes burning with determination.

Chapter Eight

Torvi and Helena watched eagerly as Jason carefully mixed up a special elixir, filling the glass to the brim.

"Here," Jason said, handing it to Torvi. "This concoction is one of the quickest ways to get drunk. Once she takes this, there's no chance she'll remain sober," he explained.

"Wait a minute Jason," Helena said, frowning. "How do you know this?"

"Er... can we not talk about it right now?" Jason asked, avoiding Helena's gaze.

"And why not? I serve drinks, and I never knew about this, but you do?"

"Okay, okay, Helena, can we let this go for now? We have a situation at hand," Torvi pleaded.

"Fine, I'll let this go for now, but you're going to have to tell me soon, I mean real soon," she emphasized, pinching Jason's ear.

"Ouch is that what I get for helping?" he grinned, rubbing his ear.

"Okay, let's go then," Torvi said, holding the glass carefully in her hands.

"Hold on. We can't all go in there. She'll suspect something is up. I think it's best if one of us goes," Jason suggested.

"Oh okay, I'll go then; you both can wait at the door in case anything happens," Torvi said, already leading the way.

"Wait Torvi; I have a better idea." Helena declared, stopping her. "I think it's best if I take the drink to her. I can make it seem like I'm betraying you. Then I'll try to make her an offer that she can't resist."

"What kind of offer? To sell me out?" Torvi demanded.

"Exactly! You got it just right." Helena beamed. "I can tell her that I'm ready to sell you out if she promises I'll partake in the magic of immortality too."

"But... I don't know if it's a..." Torvi hesitated, unsure about the whole idea.

"Trust me, Torvi; it's just to make everything sound convincing to her, okay?" Helena reassured her.

Torvi locked eyes with Helena and saw genuine sincerity in them. The notion of Ann being a spy for Raul terrified her, but she was certain that Helena would never betray her.

"I trust you, Helena. Be careful, okay?"

"Of course. You two can come with me but try to be as quiet as you can. We don't want to arouse her suspicions."

"I understand, and oh, don't forget the keys," Torvi called out. She removed the keys from her back pocket and handed them to Helena.

As Helena led the way, Torvi and Jason tiptoed behind her. When they reached the restroom door, Helena put her hand on her lips, reminding them to stay silent. Holding the drink carefully in her right hand, she took the keys from her pocket, inserted them into the lock, and turned it open. Taking one last glance at Torvi and Jason, she pushed the door and stepped inside.

Ann's eyes opened in fright as soon as she heard the door open. She looked eagerly at the door; her expression curious when she saw Helena with the glass of drink in her hands. Quickly, she began to make muffled sounds, shoving her tied hands in front of her.

"Shush! You can't let anyone know I'm in here," Helena whispered, placing her index finger on her lips and pretending to listen through the door.

Her trick worked. Ann became quiet instantly, staring wide-eyed at the door.

"Ann, I need you to listen to me, okay? I have an offer that will benefit us both. I just need you to stay quiet and hear me out. Is that clear?"

Ann nodded quickly, relaxing her head against the tiled walls.

"So, I'm sure you know me as the girl who works in the showroom, but what you don't know is that Torvi is my friend," Helena began, leaning against the wall beside Ann and crossing her legs. "I know she tied you up because you found out she doesn't really belong here. Isn't that right, Ann?"

Ann nodded quickly, an eager expression on her face.

Helena smiled and knelt beside her, careful not to spill the drink.

"Torvi told me everything because she trusted me. But I want to work with you to take her to Master Raul. I have an amazing plan on how we can pull it off, but first, I am going to remove your gag so you can talk, okay?"

Helena set the drink down beside Ann and quickly loosened the gag, tossing it aside. Ann sighed in relief and looked up at Helena with gratitude.

"Thanks," she muttered.

"You're welcome," Helena smiled. "So, back to what I was saying, are you ready to work with me?"

"Are you sure you're telling me the truth, and this isn't all a trick?" Ann asked suspiciously.

"No, it's not a trick!" Helena exclaimed, shaking her head vigorously. "Listen, Ann, look at my hands," she said, sitting on the floor beside her. "I've sold off my magic, and I want it back. Delivering Torvi to Master Raul is the perfect way. I need this, just as you do."

"Really? Are you sure about that?" Ann inquired, studying Helena's face.

"I am sure I want to help you, and I need you to help me," Helena said convincingly. "Here, I figured you'd be thirsty after being gagged for a while, so I brought you a drink from the bar to help you cool off while we talk."

"You'll have to loosen my hands for me to be able to drink," Ann pointed out.

Helena hesitated for a moment, calculating her moves. Loosening Ann's hands would give her a chance to escape, but she had to risk it. There was no other way to gain her trust.

"Of course, I'll do that right away."

Quickly, Helena loosened Ann's hands then untied her legs. She knew it was a huge gamble, but she was willing to take the risk.

"Here you go; you're free now."

"Good," Ann nodded, standing up and walking towards the door.

"Hold on a sec. We haven't concluded our plans yet," Helena quickly put out her hands to stop her.

"I don't have time for games, okay? Where's Torvi right now?" Ann demanded hotly.

"Calm down, she's helping me clean up at the showroom, and she doesn't suspect a thing. We have to handle this my way, so she doesn't get away," Helena explained, trying to calm her pounding heart.

"Good, so what's the plan?" Ann asked, folding her arms.

"Aren't you going to drink something first? Plus, you don't even have your shoes on. Let me help you with that while you drink up," Helena offered.

Picking up the drink, she handed it to Ann, who took it without hesitation.

"I would have preferred water, but it's fine," she muttered, downing the drink in one gulp.

Helena's heart beat faster as she watched Ann gulp down the drink without blinking an eye. For a moment, she wondered if Jason had been wrong. She took longer than necessary to tie the shoelace, hoping to see a reaction before she finished.

Just as she was about to give up, Ann put a hand to her head, and the glass fell from her hands. She would have collapsed on top of Helena if Helena hadn't been fast enough to hold her in place.

"I feel... so... so dizzy," Ann said slowly, her eyes half-closed.

"It worked!" Helena gasped, her eyes wide with surprise. "Torvi! Jason! Come in here!" she called out.

The door flew open immediately, and Jason rushed in, followed by Torvi.

"Yes!" Jason beamed. "I knew it was going to work! I knew-"

"Don't start the celebrations yet, happy boy," Helena interrupted. "Wait until we get her home without any hurdles. Now, help me hold her."

Helena and Jason helped Ann to the showroom and settled her into a chair. Her head lolled to the side, her dark hair covering her face. Quickly, they cleaned up the showroom, arranged the glasses and put all the chairs back in their places.

"Okay, we need to go now. I wouldn't want the man making the rounds to find us here," Helena said, drying her wet hands on a towel.

"Alright, Jason and I will go ahead while you lock up," Torvi replied.

She and Jason supported Ann on either side and walked down the stairs, waiting for Helena to lock up. When Helena joined them, they began their slow journey home. Ann seemed to grow heavier with each passing second, and they took turns supporting her to give each other a break.

People around them only gave them a passing glance before turning their attention elsewhere.

"I told you no one would notice," Jason panted, his eyes shining with pride. "We're halfway home already."

"I can't wait to get home. I never knew she was this heavy," Helena complained, breathing heavily.

"Do you want me to relieve you?" Torvi asked, turning to look back at them.

"Not yet; I can hold on for a few more minutes."

Just then, Torvi saw Caden walking towards them, just like he had the previous day.

"Helena," she called softly, slowing down a little so they walked side by side. "Caden's approaching us. He's coming straight at us," she muttered.

"Oh, do you think he might recognize her?" Jason asked worriedly.

"He certainly will!" Helena declared. "She works for Master Raul. There's no way he wouldn't know her."

"Perhaps he won't," Torvi said thoughtfully.

"You think so? Remember you told me that Caden is Master Raul's favorite guard?"

"Yes, but from what I've gathered, Master Raul is a shrewd man who enjoys making people believe they are his only confidants, so they trust him completely. I'm certain Caden has no idea there's another spy in the city keeping an eye on things."

"I hope you are right, Torvi. I really hope you are right."

They all fell silent, fixing their gazes ahead as Caden passed by. Torvi stuck close to Helena's side, watching him from the corner of her eye. His gaze followed them closely, lingering on each of their faces, giving extra attention to Ann, but he didn't say a word.

Jason turned to Torvi with a broad smile. "You were right; he doesn't seem to recog-"

"Shush!" Torvi interrupted, putting a finger to her lips. She remembered how Caden had passed them the previously and then returned. She had a feeling he might pull the same stunt, and she didn't want him overhearing anything they had to say.

After they had walked a little further without him coming back to stop them, Torvi laughed, feeling relieved. "Phew! I think he truly didn't recognize her."

"Yes, he stared right at her but didn't know who she was," Helena agreed. "I guess you are right. Raul does keep his little orderlies from knowing one another. Clever devil indeed!"

"Yes, and once we get home, I am going to tell you about my meeting with Zac today and how you two are going to help thwart Raul's plans."

"I am ready to do anything to bring that evil man down," Helena declared, anger in her voice.

"Me too, Torvi," Jason added. "You can count me in."

RAUL ASCENDED THE STAIRS with slow, deliberate steps, his slippers making no sound as he walked. He wore a flowing blue robe with spacious pockets, and his long hair cascaded freely down his back.

At the top of the stairs, he paused to listen for a moment before heading to Zac's room, which was the first on his right. Leaning in, he cupped his ear to the door but heard nothing. He gently turned the handle, his face tense with concentration. The door opened silently, and Raul tiptoed into the room, scanning every corner. He wasn't looking for anything specific, but he wanted to ensure his son wasn't planning to sabotage his big day tomorrow.

The magic of possession, which would lead to immortality, was too crucial to risk. With only three days left to live, Raul was desperate. He wasn't ready to die, not when he had barely enjoyed his rule over the city. Failure meant death, and that wasn't an option.

He hadn't confided in anyone about it, and he didn't want to. The mere thought of it terrified him. Although he hadn't seen Zac making any obvious attempts to thwart his plans, he couldn't be too sure.

Carefully, Raul made his way to Zac's wardrobe, gently opened it and searched through all the coats and shirts, checking the pockets. Finding nothing, he moved to the bathroom and inspected it thoroughly.

Satisfied that his son wasn't hiding anything, he tiptoed back to the door and quietly closed it behind him.

Zac opened his eyes and grinned. He had been awake, thinking about his plans for the next day, when he heard someone quietly opening his door. Quickly, he pretended to be deeply asleep, even adding a little snore for effect. The thought of his father snooping around his room was both surprising and amusing.

Sitting up in bed, Zac stared thoughtfully at the door, a sad look in his eyes. He loved his father and wished deep in his heart that he would change his mind. But it was clear that wasn't going to happen. Although it pained him to stop his father's plans, Zac knew he had to do it.

"THE GUEST ROOM WILL be the perfect place to keep her. The locks are strong, and she won't be able to escape through the window," Jason suggested as he and Torvi held Ann, waiting for Helena to unlock the front door.

"Yes," Helena agreed. "We don't have to tie her up as long as the door is locked." She opened the door wide for them to enter, glancing around to ensure no one was following them. Satisfied the coast was clear, she quickly locked the door behind her and hurried after Torvi and Jason.

Still holding the keys, she found the one for the guest room, opened it, and motioned for them to enter. The room was small, containing a single wardrobe and a moderate bed covered in white sheets.

"I never knew someone so lanky could weigh so much," Torvi panted as she and Jason rolled Ann onto the bed.

"Phew! Feels good to finally feel my shoulders again," Jason smiled tiredly.

The three of them stood staring at Ann for a moment. "The drink must have really knocked her out. She's deeply asleep already," Torvi observed.

"Which is great. We don't want her waking up anytime soon," Helena muttered. "Now, what about the plan? I'm so curious to know it."

"Let's go to the living room. We need to get ready soon."

"Get ready for what? Are we going out?" Jason inquired, his eyes bright with excitement.

"Yes," Torvi nodded.

She waited for Helena, and when they were all seated on the couch, she cleared her throat and began to speak.

"Zac wants you both to be part of the plan for tomorrow. He wants us all to meet at midnight so he can give us the necessary instructions."

"But where are we meeting?" Helena wondered aloud; her gaze fixed on Torvi. "Midnight is a perfect time, but still, someone is bound to notice, considering all the guards and spies Raul has combing through the city."

"We've got it all figured out, Helena," Torvi said confidently. "Once it's midnight, we just have to wait for Zac on the front steps. He'll take us to the venue."

"I'm loving the sound of this!" Jason said excitedly.

"Me too," Helena beamed. "Come on, let's go make dinner and maybe catch a couple of hours' sleep before midnight."

BY THE STROKE OF MIDNIGHT, Torvi, Helena, and Jason stood ready and waiting for Zac at the front stairs. The city lay quiet and serene, with a gentle breeze whispering around them.

"Torvi," Jason said, turning to face her. "I'm curious how Zac will take us to the venue. Can you give me a hint?"

"Patience, Jason. You'll find out soon enough," Torvi replied with a mysterious smile.

"But..." Before Jason could finish, Zac swooped down from the sky, enveloped them all in his arms, and lifted them into the air.

"Whoa! What's happening?" Jason gasped; his eyes wide as he took in the city below.

"Is this what I think it is? Am I flying?" Helena wondered, gripping Zac tightly.

"Oh yes, you're flying," Torvi laughed, recalling her own shock the first time.

"Where is he taking us?" Jason asked.

"Just wait a little longer; we'll be there soon," Torvi murmured, exchanging a glance with Zac.

As they flew, Helena and Jason bombarded Torvi with questions, and she answered as best she could. Soon, they arrived at Zac's small cottage, and he gently set them down on their feet.

The moon bathed the beautiful scenery around them in a soft glow, adding extra charm to the white cottage.

"This is... so amazing. Where are we?" Helena gasped, looking around in awe.

"Helena, Jason, welcome to my safe haven," Zac said, smiling at them.

"You own this place? It's incredible! I've never seen anything like it," Jason gushed.

Just then, a loud growl echoed from the trees, and White emerged, his eyes glowing as he stared at the newcomers.

"Oh no, what's that bear doing here?" Jason asked, terrified, as he quickly stepped behind Zac.

"Don't worry, it is just White," Torvi said, stepping forward. She knelt and opened her arms wide, and White came willingly to her, much to the astonishment of Helena and Jason.

"Run along, White. We have lots of planning to do, okay?" Zac said, gently tapping White.

"Right, come on in. We need to finish quickly so I can get you all back before people start to wake up," he said, striding toward the cabin.

"Something unexpected happened at the showroom," Torvi said, walking beside him.

"What happened? Are you alright?" Zac asked, his eyes filled with concern.

"Everything is fine. We handled the situation and have her locked up in Helena's guest room."

"What? Who?" Zac asked, his face a mix of surprise and worry.

"Ann. Remember the lady I told you about when I first came here? She turned out to be one of your father's spies and discovered who I was," Torvi explained.

"My father has a spy? I can't believe the lengths he'd go to for his greedy aims." Zac shook his head as he opened the door for them all.

"Are you sure she can't get out of the room?" he asked, turning to Jason and Helena.

"She can't get out," Jason answered confidently.

"There's nothing she can use to escape. She'll still be there when we get back," Helena added.

"Good. We need to keep her there until our plan is in motion. We can't risk her telling my father everything."

Helena and Jason went inside, leaving Torvi outside with Zac. As she walked past him, he caught her wrist and pulled her close, wrapping his arms around her.

"I missed you, Torvi," he whispered, hugging her tightly.

"I missed you too, Zac."

Zac brought his face down and tried to kiss her, but Torvi quickly moved away.

"My friends are waiting for us inside," she said, motioning to the cottage with her head.

"I know, just a quick kiss. It won't take long, I promise," Zac pleaded.

"Okay, just a brief kiss," she chuckled.

Zac tilted her head and brushed his lips over hers, barely touching.

"Is that it?" Torvi asked, disappointment in her eyes.

"You wanted it brief, right? There you have it," Zac teased, watching her face.

"Yes, but I never said..." Zac cut her off by crashing his lips to hers before she could finish her sentence. His arms tightened around her, then went down to her butt and cupped her firmly to him as he deepened the kiss.

"Zac!" Torvi gasped, pushing him away when his fingers went up her nipples and kneaded them.

"Mmhmm, I couldn't resist," he muttered, pouting his lips. Torvi pretended to want to kiss him again, but when he leaned in, she bit his lower lip softly.

"That's for trying to turn me on when my friends are just around the corner," she whispered, teasing him with her tongue.

"Ouch! Don't worry, I'll get my payback," he laughed, leading her inside.

They found Helena and Jason admiring the simple living room.

"You've got a great place here. I'd love to spend some of my afternoons here," Jason said wistfully.

"When all of this is over, I can bring you along sometime," Zac offered.

"Woah! Really, you'd do that?" Jason asked, staring at him in disbelief.

"Of course," Zac nodded. "Jason, I'd like to know what your magic gift is before we proceed. It will help me finalize my plans."

"I can control the wind. Will that work?" Jason asked eagerly.

"Oh, it's perfect!" Zac declared, patting Jason on the back. "Your ability to control the wind will suit my purpose just fine. Now, the wedding will take place in the castle's open arena. Although no one has seen it, my father had it added to the castle just for this purpose. It's built like an open field without a roof, just like typical arenas we see all around.

"For the magic of possession to take place, candles must be lit in a circle around the arena. This is where the lamp containing all the magic gifts will be kept. As I told Torvi, the lamp has a protection spell, and no one from this city can approach it except my father."

"Oh, so only Torvi can access it, right?" Helena asked, nodding in amazement.

"Yes," Zac confirmed. "Only Torvi can access it, but there will be guards all around."

"If there are guards all around, how can she get to the lamp?" Jason wondered out loud.

"This is where you and your sister come in. You two will serve as a distraction."

"Distraction?"

"Yes, Jason. I will sneak you into the castle once all the guards are gathered at the arena. Once inside, I will lead you to a room close to the arena. This room has a small window facing the arena."

"And?" Jason was so eager he couldn't keep still.

"And this is where your powers come in," Zac grinned.

"What will I do?" Jason asked.

"Take a wild guess, Jason. What do you think you can do to distract them and stop my father from casting his spells?"

Jason didn't need to think for long. It came to him instantly. "I will send a strong wind in their direction and blow out the candles," he stated, grinning at Zac.

"You got it right," Zac gushed, rubbing his head happily.

"So where do I come in then?" Helena asked, fixing her gaze on Zac.

"Helena, you will serve as another distraction."

"Okay? How? I've got no powers."

"I know," Zac said gently. "For this, you don't need to have any powers. Once Jason has confused them by blowing out the candles, I will bring you out from your hiding place. You will pretend to try to force your way in from the front of the arena. You will shout and scream about what an evil man my father is and how you can't allow him to continue unless he lets you take part in it."

"But won't he ask the guards to seize me?" Helena frowned.

"Of course, he will ask the guards to stop you, and that's exactly what I want."

"Oh, okay, so?"

"So, I will need you to put up a whole lot of struggle when they try to take you away. Scream, cry, anything to keep their attention on you," Zac instructed.

"Okay, I think I can do that," Helena smiled.

"Good. While you do all you can to keep their attention on you, I'll fly to the front of the castle where Torvi will be ready and waiting for me."

"What will I do?" Torvi asked, relieved that it was finally her turn.

"I'll pick you up from the front of the castle, fly to the arena, and put you down right where the lamp is."

"And then I smash it, right?"

"Yes, you'll pick it up and smash it to the ground. All the magic trapped inside will return to its rightful owners."

"That sounds so easy," Torvi smiled.

"It might not be as easy as it sounds. You'll have to be fast. Leave no room for the guards or my father to stop you. Hopefully, they'll be too occupied and confused with the candles going out and Helena screaming her lungs out."

"What if I'm caught after breaking the lamp?" Torvi inquired worriedly.

"I'll never allow that to happen. I'll be there to take you away before any of them recover from their shock and try to apprehend you."

"And what about me? How will I get away from the guards?" Helena asked, looking from Zac to Torvi.

"Do you have salt at home?" Zac asked, turning to Helena.

"Yes, but I don't see the connection?"

"Okay, so Jason, once you see me grab Torvi, I will need you to bring out a pack of salt and blow it in all directions. Make sure you spread it wide, so it gets into the faces of the guards and everyone else around. Helena, you will keep your eyes down while he does this, and then you can both find your way out of the castle. The salt will sting their eyes and temporarily blind them, giving us enough time to meet in front of the castle. I can then fly you all back here until everything settles down."

"You've thought of everything, haven't you?" Torvi asked, her face flushed with pride as she looked up at him.

"Well, I just hope everything goes according to plan. Besides, none of this would have been possible without you," Zac muttered, gazing into her eyes.

"I have a feeling everything will be perfect," she replied.

Their eyes locked, and Torvi felt her heart pound with all the love she felt for him. She didn't want to think about what would happen once it was all over. She knew she didn't belong in their world, but she had come to love it so much, and the thought of leaving filled her with sadness.

She had discovered love and true friendship here, in this distant city, far away from her everyday reality. The question lingered: should she give it all up and go back to her mundane life, or should she remain here forever? Thoughts of her family back in the real world came to her mind, and she sighed, wondering if she was willing to give them up to stay in this enchanting city. Unable to find answers to her many questions, she deliberately pushed them aside and focused on what was ahead of her.

Chapter Nine

"I'm so nervous, Torvi. What if something goes wrong and the plan fails?" Helena asked, pacing the living room.

"I'm nervous too," Torvi muttered, walking up to her. "But we just have to follow through with the plan and hope everything goes well."

Zac had brought them back to the house, and although it was still a few hours before dawn, they were all too anxious to sleep. While Torvi and Helena were nervous, Jason was overly excited and couldn't keep still. He kept clenching and unclenching his hands as he sat on the couch.

"I haven't used my powers in months!" he exclaimed, smacking his hands together. "I can't wait to use them to defeat Master Raul. He doesn't know what's coming for him." He grinned at the two ladies, but they were not in the same jolly mood.

"Come on, you two need to relax, okay?" he said, walking over to put his arms around them. "If you get too worked up, you'll be too jittery to carry out the plan effectively."

"I know," Torvi admitted. "It's just that from what I know about Raul, he's very clever, and he might have something else up his sleeve."

"No, he won't," Jason said with conviction.

"How can you be so sure?" Helena asked, frowning at him.

"Come, sit," he led them both to the couch and sat between them. "Helena, I know you don't like me talking about my days in the gambling world, but there's something I learned there."

"Okay, and what's that?" Helena asked, folding her arms.

"Well, from what I've gathered about Master Raul, he's like one of those clever people I knew back then. One thing they do is underestimate everyone else. They think everyone else is stupid, so after they make their careful plans, they relax, believing that no one else will be clever enough to uncover their plans.

"Unknown to them, there are people way cleverer than they are, and, in this case, Zac is steps ahead of his father. It takes a genius to come up with such an amazing plan, and the way he thought of every detail, down to how we were going to escape from the castle, is just brilliant. Until tonight, I would never have considered salt to be such a powerful weapon. So, you two need to stop being overly nervous, okay? Everything is going to be just great," he finished, beaming at them.

"Who would have thought a young chap like you could give such motivation?" Helena said, pinching his ear.

"I would never have thought he was capable of it," Torvi teased. "And you know what?" she continued, turning to smile at Jason. "I feel a whole lot better and motivated already, thank you."

"I feel better, too," Helena nodded. "I think we should get some sleep. We need to be alert for the task ahead of us."

"Yes, I agree." Torvi nodded, rising to her feet. "I think I should check on Ann and see if she's awake."

"It's better we all go together," Helena suggested. "If she's conscious, she might try to attack you to escape, but she won't be able to get past the three of us."

"You're right. Let's go," Torvi said, leading the way.

As they approached the guestroom, Jason tapped Helena and Torvi, signaling them to stop.

"I think we need to tie her up again. She might still be weak and have a throbbing headache from the elixir, but in a few hours, she'll regain her strength and might scream, drawing people's attention."

"Jason is right," Helena said, turning to look at Torvi.

"But she'll be so uncomfortable and stiff," Torvi pointed out, looking worried.

"I know, but there's no other way," Helena insisted. "It's just for a day, okay? We'll find a way to feed her once it's dawn, and then tie her back up. Once our mission is accomplished, we can let her go."

"All right, I guess we just have to do it." Torvi agreed a bit reluctantly.

"Great, you two wait here while I get a rope and a piece of cloth to gag her," Jason said, quickly walking off.

"She doesn't deserve your pity," Helena muttered when she saw the sad look in Torvi's eyes. "She wouldn't have hesitated to tell Raul everything if she had the chance. She knows what he's doing is wrong, but she doesn't care as long as it benefits her in some way. Don't worry about her, okay?"

Torvi nodded just as Jason returned with a long rope and a piece of cloth. "Let's go," he said, leading the way this time.

Ann was still sleeping when they got to the room. She lay sprawled on the bed, her dark hair covering her face.

"She must have been zonked out pretty badly," Helena whispered.

"Yes," Jason whispered back, approaching the bed. "I'll just tie her hands while you tie her legs."

Helena took the shorter rope from Jason and walked quietly to the end of the bed while Torvi held the piece of cloth. Just as Jason took Ann's hands and tried to put them together, she turned around so quickly and struck out with her fist, almost hitting his face.

"Oh no!" Torvi gasped, rushing to the bed. "She's been awake all this time!"

"You let me go right now!" Ann yelled, struggling to get off the bed but Helena held her feet firmly.

Torvi quickly jumped onto the bed, grabbing Ann's swinging hands and pinning them together. Ann twisted and turned trying to free herself, but with Helena holding her feet and Torvi holding her hands, her struggle was futile.

"Tie up her hands first!" Torvi commanded, struggling to keep Ann's hands together. Jason swung into action. He moved beside Torvi and secured the rope firmly around Ann's wrists.

"You won't get away with this!" Ann yelled, trying to yank her hands free.

"Quit struggling!" Torvi snapped, holding tightly to Ann's wrists as Jason bound them. "You brought this upon yourself, and there's nothing you can do now."

"Jason, hurry!" Helena panted, her chest heaving as she fought to keep Ann's legs in her grip.

"Just a few seconds Helena, I'm almost done," Jason called out.

As Jason rushed over to Helena's side, Ann opened her mouth and let out a blood-curdling scream that took them all by surprise. Torvi stood frozen in shock for a couple of seconds, but she quickly snapped out of it. In one fast move, she grabbed the cloth she had left on the bed and tied it over Ann's mouth, muffling her screams.

Ann began to kick wildly, moving all over the bed, but Helena and Jason had her held down tightly, and in no time they had her legs firmly tied. The fight drained from Ann as soon as they finished tying her up. She lay still, completely silent, her chest rising and falling with heavy breaths.

"Phew! That was a whole... a whole lot of work," Helena panted, stepping away from the bed and leaning against the wall.

"Yes, who knew she could be so fierce," Torvi sighed, shaking her head as she stared at Ann lying on the bed.

"Do you think anyone heard her?" Jason asked, worry etched on his face.

"I hope not," Helena replied, closing her eyes. "It's still way too early for anyone to be awake, so there's good chance no one heard her."

"To think that I was feeling pity for her," Torvi spat, glaring at Ann on the bed.

"I told you she didn't deserve it," Helena muttered, walking over to Torvi and taking her hand. "Let's go, she's securely tied up, and there's no way she can escape."

Torvi and Jason sat on the couch as soon as they reached the living room, while Helena stretched out on the largest couch.

"I still think we should get some sleep. I'm already exhausted, and I still have to get up early for the showroom," she muttered sleepily.

"I need to sleep too," Jason yawned, standing up. "I'll see you both later."

"All right, Jason, I'll just be here," Torvi said.

She leaned back against the couch and watched Helena doze off. Torvi wished she could sleep too, but her mind was too occupied. She worried about the plan, about Zac, about Ann and everyone else, but most importantly, she was worried about her heart.

Zac had made her fall completely in love with him, and the uncertainty of the future made everything more complicated. She knew she couldn't stay in the city forever. She belonged in the real world, but what would happen if she chose to stay? Would there be consequences for her, or could she just remain with the man she loved? Unable to find an answer, she curled up on the couch. Her eyes closed on their own accord, and she drifted into a calm, peaceful sleep.

A LOUD KNOCK JOLTED Torvi and Helena awake at dawn. Wide-eyed, they exchanged glances, sleep vanishing as they wondered who could be at the door. Helena put a finger to her lips and motioned for Torvi to go into the other room while she investigated. Torvi nodded and tiptoed away, careful not to make a sound.

Taking a deep breath, Helena approached the door and peered through the peephole. A middle-aged man dressed in old, faded clothes stood there, his hands tucked into his coat pockets.

"Yes, how may I help you, sir?" Helena asked, opening the door just an inch.

"Oh, good morning, miss. Sorry to bother you," the man greeted with a warm smile, but Helena remained unmoved.

"Good morning, sir. Is there a problem?" she inquired, scanning the surroundings.

"No, not at all," the man replied, shaking his head. "I was taking a walk just before dawn and thought I heard some muffled yelling coming from your place. I just wanted to make sure everything was alright."

"Oh, that? It's nothing serious," Helena forced out a chuckle. "You see, my brother and I were having a silly fight over a chocolate bar. He pulled my hair, and I yelled. Very silly, right?" she said, trying to make her laughter sound genuine.

"Ah yes, very silly indeed," the man nodded, attempting to peer inside, but Helena stood her ground.

"If that's all, sir, I'd like to go back inside now," she announced, watching his expression closely.

"Yes, that's all," the man nodded. "I was just concerned when I heard the strange noises and, err, decided to check."

"Thank you so much. We're perfectly fine," Helena said, forcing a smile. "Goodbye and have a great day."

Locking the door firmly behind her, she deliberately stamped her feet on the ground, creating the illusion of walking away. After a few seconds, she crept back to the door, peeking through the peephole again. The man was still there, staring curiously at the house.

"Who was that?" Torvi asked, as she walked into the living room, with Jason close behind.

"Some man," Helena replied, approaching them.

"What did he want?" Torvi and Jason asked in unison.

"He claims he heard muffled cries earlier and came to check if we were all right, but I don't believe him for a second. It seems like he works with Ann."

"What? Are you sure?" Jason asked, quickly peeking through the door, but the man was gone.

"I'm positive. The way he looked at the house, it was as if he knew something, but I'm not sure."

"We have to be stay alert; he might be another spy working for Raul," Torvi stated. "Maybe he saw us coming home with Ann and decided to hang around."

"Yes, we must be on guard. Right, I need to get to the showroom," Helena said, leaving the living room.

"How about we make a quick breakfast, then go check on Ann?" Torvi suggested, turning to Jason.

"Sounds great. Let's do it," Jason agreed, leading the way to the kitchen.

ZAC WENT ABOUT HIS usual activities in the castle, maintaining a calm and unbothered demeanor as he sat down for breakfast with his father. For many years, his father had never joined him at the dining table, and Zac couldn't fathom his reason to do so that morning.

"What are your plans for today, Zac?" Raul asked, taking a sip of his coffee.

Zac's fork paused midway to his mouth, and he quickly looked up from his scrambled eggs, eyes widening in surprise as he stared at his father.

"Why are you asking? Is there a problem?"

"No, not at all. Is it wrong for a father to want to know about his son's activities?" Raul asked, spreading his arms wide.

"Err... No, it's just that you and I stopped having that father-and-son relationship a long time ago," Zac replied, watching his father's expression closely.

"I know, son, but I want things to change between us," Raul said convincingly, reaching out to touch Zac's hand on the table. "I want to be part of your life from now on, and I want you to be part of mine too."

"Really?" Zac asked, momentarily believing his father's words.

"Yes," Raul nodded, a smile spreading across his face. "Speaking of being in your life, how long have you been with that woman? I've never seen her with you before."

Zac stared into his father's eyes and smiled. For a moment, he had almost been fooled into believing that his father was genuinely interested in his life. But he quickly realized his father only wanted information, to know if he had any idea about what would happen at midnight, and to find out who Torvi really was. Deciding to play along, he gave his father the answer he wanted to hear.

"I've known her for a while now, father," he replied, sipping his coffee.

"Why have I never seen her with you before?" Raul inquired.

"Because I didn't want to make my relationship with her public. But since you were trying to force me to marry Fiya, I had to let everyone know that I already have a woman. As for my plans for today, I think I'll just lie in bed this morning. I don't feel like working," he explained with conviction in his voice.

"Oh great," Raul beamed, pushing back his chair and standing up. "Make sure you rest well and spend time with your woman later. It's a bright, beautiful day for lovers."

"Thank you, father. I will do just that."

Zac chuckled softly to himself as Raul walked out of the room. Only a fool would believe his father, and he was no fool. The time was drawing nearer, and oh, he just couldn't wait.

AS NIGHT FELL, TORVI and Jason made their way to the showroom. They walked with their hands clasped tightly, too anxious for small talk. The day had felt interminable to Torvi; each hour dragging by slowly. Now, walking through the brightly lit city with Jason's hand in hers, she struggled to hide her nervousness. Every stare, every laugh and every whisper seemed suspicious to her. It felt as though everyone was watching them more closely than usual, and every man in faded clothes seemed to be tracking their every move.

She knew she was imagining things, but her anxiety was too overwhelming to control her thoughts. A glance at Jason confirmed he was nervous too; his eyes darted around as they walked, and he tensed whenever anyone got too close.

As they neared the showroom, they quickened their pace, eager to get inside. They planned to enter through the back door, which Helena had promised to leave open. As they approached the side of the building, Torvi suddenly stopped and smiled at Jason.

"Jason, everything is going to be fine, okay?" she assured him, gripping both his hands.

"Yes, I believe so," he replied, returning her smile.

"Let's go." Torvi said, as they walked up the stairs.

Inside, they found Helena pacing the corridor, waiting anxiously for them.

"Finally, what took you both so long?" Helena asked as soon as she saw them.

"We waited until everyone left the showroom," Torvi explained.

"I was so worried. I thought something had happened," Helena muttered leading them through the corridor to the main room.

"Everything is fine. We stayed inside, and no one else came to the house," Jason assured her.

"What about Ann?" Helena asked, glancing at them.

"Ann's fine. It was challenging to feed her and help her to the restroom, but we managed," Torvi replied.

The showroom's front doors were tightly shut, and all the windows closed. Torvi sat in a chair, gently tapping on the floor with her boots.

"So, what do we do before Zac comes to get us?" Jason asked, looking from Torvi to Helena.

"Nothing. He said he would come once the half-moon was in the sky. He wants them to start the ritual so he can sneak us into the castle without interruptions. We just have wait for his whistle, which will be the sign for us to come outside," Torvi answered.

"I want us to stay as silent as possible," Helena whispered, sitting next to Torvi. "Although the man in charge of making the rounds doesn't come often, I don't want us to make too much noise. Someone might wonder why people are still in the showroom after closing time."

"All right," Torvi and Jason nodded.

They sat in silence, watching as the clock ticked by slowly. As the city grew quiet, so did their apprehension. Shortly before midnight, they clasped hands and stared at the big clock on the wall, their hearts beating fast as they waited for Zac's whistle.

"Are you sure he's still coming? What if his father did something to stop him?" Jason asked, his eyes filled with worry.

Torvi thought about the smart, resilient man she had fallen hopelessly in love with and smiled, confident that Zac would find a way out of any situation. "He's going to come," she said firmly. "Just hold on for a few more minutes."

"Okay," Jason nodded, taking a deep breath. "I'm just wondering if Raul might have started the whole thing before we got..."

Jason's words trailed off as a soft whistle came from the back of the building.

"Yes! He's here!" Jason exclaimed, jumping to his feet.

"I told you," Torvi grinned.

"Phew!" Helena sighed, placing her hand on her chest. "I guess it's time; let's not keep him waiting."

Torvi led the way, and as they walked down the corridor her heartbeat quickened. She hadn't seen Zac all day, and she missed him terribly. She paused when she saw him standing on the first step, dressed in a long blue coat, his dark hair blowing around him, and his sword at his side.

His face broke into a wide smile when he saw her. He opened his arms, and Torvi eagerly went into them, sighing as he hugged her close.

"Jason, Helena," he beamed, clasping them each in a side hug without letting go of Torvi.

"Hi Zac, I was worried something had happened to you and you wouldn't show up," Jason said.

"Yes, I was worried too, just didn't voice it," Helena confessed, sounding relieved.

"There's nothing to worry about," Zac assured them. "Everything is going to go smoothly, okay?"

"Okay," Jason and Helena answered in unison.

"Do you all remember our plans?" Zac asked, looking at each of them in turn.

"Yup, I know I am to put a great struggle and shout as much as I can," Helena answered, grinning.

"And I have my pack of salt right here," Jason said, tapping a bulge in the pocket of his coat.

"Perfect, perfect!" Zac grinned, feeling happy. "We are going to succeed; you know why? Because we are doing this for the good of everyone. No matter what anyone thinks, good always transcends evil, and I am certain we will succeed tonight. Remember, no matter what happens, we have to stick to the plan."

They all nodded, feeling much more energized and encouraged. Zac glanced around, ensuring no one was lurking shadows. He wrapped his arms around them all and soared into the sky.

ZAC FOUND IT EASY TO sneak Jason and Helena into the castle. As he had guessed, there were no guards around; they were all gathered at the arena, allowing him to move about freely without interruptions.

First, he took Helena to a spot behind the arena where his father's large sculpture provided ample cover. All the guards had their backs turned to her, giving her an unrestricted view of the surroundings.

"Stay here and wait until all the candles are blown out," he instructed, crouching beside her.

"Yes, I understand," she nodded, then turned to Jason, drawing him close. "Hey brother, make sure you blow out every single candle, okay?"

"I will blow out everything with all my might," Jason muttered, tears filling his eyes as he stared at Helena's face. "I hope with all my heart our plan succeeds so you can get your magic back. I'm so sorry for all the pain I caused you, sorry for making you sell your magic to save..."

"Shush," Helena said, placing a hand on his arm. "Now is not the time, okay? You are my brother, and I love you with all my heart. Now go and make me proud, okay?"

"Okay," Jason nodded, blinking back his tears.

"Time to go, Jason," Zac said quietly.

"Bye," Jason whispered, turning to take one last glance at Helena before Zac whisked him away.

"Bye for now. I hope when I see you again, I will have my magic back," Helena said, her eyes filling with tears as she watched her brother go.

Zac produced a set of keys from his pocket and carefully opened the door to the small room facing the arena. He quickly surveyed the room before motioning to Jason to follow him. The room was small, barely enough for the two of them. A small round window provided a clear view of the arena's center. Zac and Jason watched the scene in front of them in awe, their eyes taking in every detail.

Candles of various colors burned brightly, their flames flickering. Guards surrounded the arena, their hands resting on their swords, ready for action. In the middle of the candles stood Fiya and Caden, staring at each other. They were both dressed in long red robes with hoods, completely covering their heads and hair. The oversized robes cascaded down to the floor, giving the impression they were floating inside them.

Master Raul, dressed in a long red coat that swept the floor, walked around the circle. His silver hair flowed freely, and he held a book and a short rope. After circling twice, he began to tie Caden's hands.

"Listen, I need you to remain unseen, okay?" Zac whispered, gripping Jason's shoulders. "Stay low and watch everything they do. Be alert and don't get distracted.

"When my father starts chanting from the book and circling the candles, I need you to blow them out immediately, Jason. Make sure you're not seen; our escape plan depends on it. And remember, you need to blow the salt into their eyes before we can go."

"Don't worry, Zac. I know how important this is, and I'll give it my all. Thousands of lives depend on it, and I know how hard you've planned everything. I won't fail you." Jason assured him.

"Thanks, Jason," Zac said, touched by his words. "I'll see you soon."

As soon as Zac left the room, Jason crouched on the floor and pulled the pack of salt from his pocket. Using his teeth, he tore the wrapping as quietly as he could, opened the bag wide, and placed it beside him on the floor. He wanted everything to be ready so he could act quickly.

Zac flew back to the front of the castle, where Torvi was hiding in a corner. She whirled around at the sound of footsteps, relaxing only when she saw Zac.

"How's it all going?" she asked, looking up at him.

"Everything is going according to plan," Zac replied, drawing her into his arms and kissing the top of her head. "Helena and Jason are already in position; I just came to check up on you one last time before I go back inside."

"Okay, I'm happy everything is going well," she said, smiling brightly at him.

"My darling, is something bothering you? You don't seem too happy," Zac observed, looking into her eyes.

"I'm just thinking," Torvi whispered, holding him tightly.

"About what?"

"Thinking about what will happen when all of this is over."

"I've been thinking about it too," Zac sighed, kissing her gently.

"Let's not worry about it now. We have a mission at hand, and I'm sure we'll figure something out," Torvi said, trying to sound cheerful.

"You're a wonderful person, Torvi, and I love you with all my heart. I hope we find a way when this is all over," he whispered, lowering his head to capture her lips with his.

Torvi wrapped her arms around him, nearly weeping from the sheer joy of being in his embrace. She pushed aside every thought of leaving, choosing instead to focus on the present and bask in the love of the man who had filled her heart completely.

"Go back inside," she whispered, her breath heavy as she broke the kiss.

"I hate to leave you out here alone, but it will be easier for me to fly you into the arena from here," Zac said reluctantly.

"Don't worry, I'll be fine," Torvi reassured him.

"I need you to have this," Zac said, reaching into his pocket and pulling out a small bottle filled with a red, watery substance.

"What's this?" Torvi asked, looking curiously at the object as she took it from his hands.

"It's pepper spray. I need you to hold onto it, just in case," Zac said.

"Okay, thanks," Torvi replied.

"Alright, darling, stay low, okay? I'll see you soon." Zac gave her one final kiss before striding away.

Torvi tucked the bottle into her coat pocket and sighed, already missing Zac.

Just as she was about to lean against one of the pillars, she heard footsteps behind her. Her heart raced as she quickly turned around. Standing before her was the burly man who had spilled his drink on her at the showroom.

Chapter Ten

Zac found a perfect spot behind a pillar at the arena and waited, his heart pounding with anticipation. He watched his father walk around the circle, the book open in his arms. His eyes checked the spot where Jason was waiting, and he sighed, hoping everything would go smoothly. Folding his arms across his chest, he decided all he could do was wait.

Jason kept his gaze fixed on the arena, not wanting to miss anything. He rubbed his palms together, eager to unleash the powers he had kept unused for so long. He could see the lamp in the middle, its glow mingling with that of the candles. Taking a deep breath, he put his hands together and waited patiently for the right moment to strike.

Raul stared at Caden and Fiya with satisfaction; a small smile spreading across his face. Raising his face to the sky, he studied the moon for a while, lifted the book towards it for a couple of seconds, and then brought it down. Taking a deep breath, he fixed his gaze on the book and began to cast spells, walking around the circle.

As Raul chanted, Jason closed his eyes and opened his palms, summoning the winds into them. He positioned his hands to face both sides of the arena, ensuring the wind came from all directions. After a few seconds, he directed the wind towards the candles, extinguishing their flames.

Raul's eyes widened in shock as the candles suddenly went out. His mouth hung open as he looked around, trying to decipher the source of the wind.

"No, no," he gasped, moving from one extinguished candle to another. "This can't be happening, not now!"

His voice trembled, and his hands shook with fury as he scanned the arena. Caden, Fiya, and the guards also looked around, unable to determine where the wind had come from.

"Can't you just relight the candles?" Caden asked.

"Do you think it's that easy?" Raul spat, his eyes blazing with anger as he stared at Caden. "A spell must be recited thirty minutes in advance for the candles to function."

"But can't you start..."

"Just shut up!" Raul yelled, cutting Caden off. "Shut your mouth before I shut it for you!"

"Guards," he roared, pointing a shaking finger at them. "Don't just stand there like confused idiots; find out who did this!"

As the guards were about to disperse, Helena emerged from her hiding place and rushed towards Raul. The guards, stunned by her sudden appearance, froze momentarily but quickly recovered before she reached Raul.

"You evil man with a dark, dark heart!" Helena screamed; her breath heavy as she struggled against the guards holding her on both sides. "I won't let this happen. I will not allow you to proceed with your plan unless you let me partake in the magic of possession that grants immortality."

Raul threw his head back and let out a loud, mocking laugh, a deadly look in his eyes as he approached Helena.

"Who are you, and how did you find this place?" he yelled angrily, grabbing her by the neck.

"I... I want to be part of your magic," Helena huffed, her chest heaving. "You have to allow me to partake in the magic of possession. That is the only way I will tell you how I got in here."

Raul stared at her closely, a puzzled expression on his face. He glanced around the arena, searching for anything unusual, but everything seemed the same. Shaking his head, he turned his attention back to Helena.

"How did you know about the magic of possession? Who told you?" he asked in a fierce whisper.

"As I said, I am not going to say a word until..."

"If you don't start talking right away, I will turn you into a frozen ice sculpture," Raul threatened, tightening his grip on her neck.

Helena's heart pounded wildly in her chest as she stared up at Raul. She had never been this close to him before. His furious, intimidating look scared her to her core, and she almost felt like dropping to her knees and confessing everything. If she didn't start talking, he might carry out his threat.

But she knew she had to keep Raul distracted until Torvi reached the lamp. Staring defiantly into his eyes, she hoped Torvi and Zac would get there soon before she lost the little courage she had left.

TORVI STOOD MOTIONLESS, momentarily stunned by the man's appearance. After a few seconds, she glanced behind him, contemplating whether he had somehow managed to get Ann out of the house. However, there was no one behind him.

She stared at the sword he held in his hands, willing herself to stay calm as different thoughts raced through her mind. Time was precious, and she couldn't afford to waste any of it. Even though she couldn't see what was happening in the arena, she guessed that Raul might have begun casting spells, and that Zac would return for her at any moment.

"Well, who do we have here?" he muttered, holding a sword to her neck.

"Who are you, and what do you want?" Torvi asked, taking a step back.

"Quit pretending!" the man snapped, anger in his voice. "I know you remember me from the showroom. As for what I want, I'm taking you into the castle and presenting you to Master Raul myself!"

"Are you one of his spies? Do you work with Ann?" Torvi asked, trying to keep the man talking as she thought of an escape plan.

"No," the man shook his head. Seeing how defenseless Torvi looked, he lowered his sword and sheathed it. "I work for Caden, but he doesn't pay me well enough. He asked me to follow you, and I've been doing that since I deliberately spilled a drink on you at the showroom.

"I knew there was something off about you. When I saw Zac with you all today, I figured he was taking you to the castle, but I couldn't figure out why. However, seeing you without your glasses on makes everything clearer."

"Oh, great story," Torvi smiled charmingly, wanting to appear perfectly harmless to the man. "Since you work for Caden, why do you want to take me to Master Raul yourself?"

"Because I want to be a part of the magic of possession. Caden wanted to know who you truly are so he could somehow use you to blackmail Raul, but right now, I'm going to use you for myself." He grinned, taking a step closer to her.

Torvi nodded agreeably and waited for him to get closer. As he gripped her arm and began to shove her towards the castle, she deliberately hit her leg against a pillar and suddenly fell backward, taking him down with her. She was back on her feet in a split second, but the man struggled to get up because of his size.

Before he could haul himself up, Torvi quickly opened the bottle Zac had given her and sprayed a generous amount directly into the man's eyes.

"You silly girl!" he grunted out in pain, clutching at his eyes.

He searched around for her; his legs unsteady as he managed to get on his feet. Torvi moved out of his way, contemplating her next move. She watched as he vigorously rubbed his eyes with his coat, trying to get the pepper spray out. Soon, he managed to open his eyes a little, but Torvi immediately sprayed another dose into them, eliciting another loud grunt of pain from him.

Torvi looked around her, hoping Zac would appear at any moment. The man was making a lot of noise, and she knew it was only a matter of time before it attracted attention from inside the castle. She heaved a sigh of relief when Zac landed in front of her, his coat blowing in the wind.

"Torvi," he gasped, taking hold of her hand. "We have to go now!" He quickly wrapped his coat around her, too rushed to notice the large man groaning on the ground in pain.

"Wait a minute," Torvi panted, pointing to the ground. "There's a man here. He works for Caden and tried to take me to Raul, but I sprayed the contents of your bottle into his eyes."

Zac whirled around, looked at the man rubbing his eyes, and shook his head.

"He doesn't matter right now," he said quickly, his voice tense. "Helena is in danger. My father is threatening to turn her into an ice sculpture if she doesn't tell him what he wants to hear. I didn't know he would try to get information from her; I thought he would just have the guards take her away. But she has his full attention. We have to get to the lamp now!"

"Okay," Torvi nodded, taking one last glance at the man on the ground before Zac took off into the sky with her.

As they flew over the arena, Torvi quickly took in the scene below. She saw Caden's hands tied together with those of a woman she assumed to be the fire princess. In the center of the candles, a lamp emitted a blue glow. All the guards and Raul were focused on Helena, and Torvi's heart pounded hard against her chest when she saw Raul's powerful hands gripping her friend's neck.

Quickly, Zac set her down five meters from them and stood waiting with his arms wide open, ready to take off with her once the lamp was broken. Hearing footsteps, Fiya turned away from Raul and looked back at the lamp. Her eyes widened in shock as she saw Torvi standing nearby.

"Raul!" Fiya screamed, her voice echoing through the silent night. "She's trying to steal the lamp!"

Raul instantly let go of Helena and turned to look at Torvi. His expression shifted to surprise when he saw Zac standing behind her, his arms outstretched. Suddenly, he erupted in loud laughter, gripping his sides.

"Bravo, bravo, bravo!" he declared, clapping his hands. "I shouldn't have taken your silence for granted. You had me fooled, didn't you, pretending as though you had nothing up your sleeve, but it was all a lie. You've been planning to stop me all along, haven't you? You are clever, Zac, just like me."

"I am nothing like you," Zac declared vehemently, angered by his father's comparison. "You are greedy, a user, and a man who wants to fulfill his own selfish desires without considering the harm to others. I won't let you take magic from the people and use it for your immortality. It's never going to happen!"

"And who is going to stop me?" Raul asked, his posture relaxed as he looked at Zac. "Her?" he asked, smirking as he pointed to Torvi, who had her head bowed so he couldn't see her eyes.

"Do you and your little lover think you can stop me after I have spent years planning? I guess I gave you more credit than you deserve, Zac. You must be a fool to believe I would leave the lamp unguarded. Anyone who touches that lamp will turn to ice immediately."

"You must be very proud of yourself, father," Zac laughed. "However, your magic cannot affect her because she's not from this world; she's from the real world."

As Zac spoke, Torvi pushed back her hair and lifted her face, revealing her eyes to everyone. The guards gasped loudly, and Raul stepped back in shock, speechless.

"You see, Father, I am always two steps ahead of you," Zac chuckled. "Torvi, do it now!" he commanded, turning to her.

Torvi quickly moved towards the lamp and went to grab it, but Raul's cry stopped her in her tracks.

"No!" Raul cried out, reaching toward Zac as he fell to the floor. "Please, son, don't do this to me," he pleaded, his voice trembling.

"What?" Zac mouthed, too stunned by his father's behavior. Raul had never been one to plead, but there he was, begging in front of his subordinates and guards.

"Please, Zac, I need this magic of immortality to stay alive," he gasped, clasping his hands together.

"What do you mean, 'to stay alive'?" Zac asked, looking at his father, confused.

Raul looked around, hesitating. Everyone in the arena had their eyes fixed on him. Taking a deep breath, he looked straight at his son.

"I... I have just a couple of days to live," he confessed, lowering his head. "Please, I am at the end of my years, and this is my only chance to live longer. Do not let her destroy the lamp. For the sake of our relationship as father and son, don't let her do it."

Zac struggled to control his emotions. A mixture of pity for his father and his quest for justice stirred in his heart. For a moment, the pity almost overwhelmed him, but he shook his head, fighting it back.

No matter how bad his father was, a part of him would always love him. But a greater part of him could not allow his father's reign to continue in the city. The people deserved better, and he would ensure they got what they deserved.

"I'm sorry, Father," he said, shaking his head. "I can't let you do this. You've lived your life to the fullest but caused much pain to the people of this city. Despite everything, I still love you, but I want a different future for the people. I want equal distribution of resources so everyone can be happy. Those who had no choice but to sell their magic gifts to you should get back what belongs to them. They shouldn't have any reason to sell because they will have more than enough once the resources are shared equally. I'm sorry, but your magic can't affect her."

"But mine can," Fiya declared in a loud, firm voice.

Torvi shifted her gaze to Fiya, watching as she flicked her fingers upward. A fire appeared, burning the rope Raul had used to tie her hand to Caden's. A proud smile spread across Fiya's face as she removed her hood, revealing her long white hair and glowing eyes.

Torvi's eyes met Zac's, and she saw that he was as confused as she was. He stared at Fiya with a frown, indecision in his eyes.

"When you were making your carefully laid out plans, I guess you forgot that the magic of fire works in both worlds," Fiya said, smiling as she rubbed her palms together. "Of all the magic gifts, fire is the strongest and most sort after. The power of a fire princess has no bounds. This is the end of the road for you, Zac. If she touches the lamp, I will make her burn!" Fiya threatened.

A wide grin suddenly appeared on Raul's face, and he instantly jumped to his feet. "How quick the twist of fate can be," he stated arrogantly. "Fiya darling, make sure you burn her to a crisp if she dares take the lamp," he commanded, turning to look at Fiya.

"Gladly, master," she chuckled, a small fire already forming in her hands.

"Torvi," Zac called, stretching his hands to her. "We have to let it go; there's nothing we can do now."

Torvi shook her head, tears filling her eyes. She couldn't believe they had gotten this far only to turn back now. Her gaze fell on Helena's face, and she saw that she, too, was in tears, no longer struggling against the guards holding her arms.

"You've been warned, Torvi," Fiya shouted, throwing her head back and taking a stance. "I will not have an ounce of pity for you once my fire begins to consume you."

"Please, let's go," Zac pleaded. "I can't let anything happen to you. I can't, Torvi." His voice shook with emotion, and tears filled his eyes.

Torvi was about to step away from the lamp when she felt a cool wind on her left cheek. Out of the corner of her eye, she saw Jason's face peeking from the window of the small room beside the arena. Winking at her, he opened his palms and looked in Fiya's direction.

Torvi instantly understood his message. Careful not to let anyone notice the direction of her gaze, she pretended to step back a little, but instead she bent and picked up the lamp.

"No!" Zac screamed in horror, his face ashen with fear. "Torvi, what are you doing?"

"You fool," Fiya snarled, her chest heaving with anger. "You asked for it!"

Fiya twisted her hands, and the fire in her palms grew larger. With a smile on her face, she sent the flames flying toward Torvi.

"No!" Zac yelled, jumping in front of the fire to shield Torvi from it. As the fire advanced, he closed his eyes and stood tall. Just before it reached him, Jason summoned a strong wind that blew the fire away from Zac and redirected it toward Raul. Raul let out a horrifying scream, and at the same time, Torvi lifted the lamp high into the sky and hurled it to the ground, smashing it into tiny little fragments.

The lamp exploded, the impact knocking Torvi to the ground. A bright blue light emanated from the lamp, before scattering in all directions. Zac stood confused for a moment, but quickly understood what had happened.

"Jason, now!" he cried out, rushing towards Torvi.

Jason, who already had the packet of salt open, quickly placed it on the window and sent it flying in all directions. Before Fiya could recover from her shock and conjure up another fire, the salt flew into her eyes and those of the guards around her. They all cried out, rubbing vigorously at their eyes.

While Jason jumped out of the window, Helena took to her heels, heading for the front of the castle with Jason close behind. By the time they reached the front of the castle, Zac was already waiting for them. Without wasting a second, Zac gathered them all in his arms and took off into the sky.

Back inside the arena, Fiya ran to where Raul lay on the ground, most of his body burned beyond recognition.

"Oh no!" she cried, kneeling beside Raul. "I'm so sorry, master, so sorry." she sobbed, placing her hands on his body.

"Fiya," Raul said weakly. "I only have a couple of days left so I won't suffer much. But I want you to do something for me."

"Anything, master," Fiya answered, lowering her ear to his head.

"Find Torvi. Take all the guards you need but make sure she doesn't return to the real world without a burn on her body. Promise me, Fiya," he muttered, gripping her hand.

"I will find her," she vowed with determination. "Even if it means burning this whole city down, I will make sure she doesn't escape."

"TORVI, CAN YOU HEAR me?" Zac called, gently tapping her cheek. They were back in his cottage, and he laid her on the rug-covered floor while Helena and Jason hovered nearby, their faces filled with worry.

Torvi slowly opened her eyes, and then smiled widely. "We did it, right?" she asked, looking from one to another.

"Yes!" Zac replied, kissing the back of her hands. "We did it! I'm so sorry for putting you in danger. I didn't realise the magic of fire could affect someone from the real world. I am so..."

"Shush," Torvi whispered, placing a hand on his lips. "We succeeded in giving people their magic back; that's all that matters right now."

"Yes," Zac nodded, pushing back happy tears. "That's all that matters."

Gently, he helped her to her feet but kept his arms around her.

"Oh, Torvi, I was so scared she was going to burn you!" Helena exclaimed, enveloping her in a deep hug.

"Not when Jason's there," Torvi chuckled, hugging Helena back. "Come here," she said, drawing Jason into the hug.

"Helena, you did an excellent job, and Jason, I can't thank you enough. You saved the night, buddy," Zac said, wrapping his arms around all of them.

"What next?" Helena asked when they broke apart. "Do we wait here until things calm down or what?"

Zac turned to look at Torvi, a sad look in his eyes. "The person in real danger right now is Torvi. Seeing what happened back at the arena, I know my father is going to try his best to hurt her before he dies. Now that he has the fire princess doing his bidding, it's only a matter of time before they find us here. We must get Torvi back to the real world," he explained.

"Is there no other way?" Jason asked, tears filling his eyes.

"Yes, we don't want her to go, at least not yet." Helena cried out, wrapping her arms around Torvi once again.

"Yes, Zac, can't I stay for a few days?" Torvi asked.

Zac's gaze met Torvi's, and the thought of not seeing her again made his heart ache. He wished for nothing more than to spend the rest of his life with her, but her safety came first. He would rather die than let anything happen to her; he had to get her home safely, that was his priority.

"I wish for nothing more than to keep you here with me, Torvi, but I can't risk you getting burned beyond recognition. Her magic transcends to the real world, so this means you will still have the burns when you get back, and it could kill you. I love you too much to allow that to happen to you."

"I understand, I do." Torvi nodded, tears streaming down her cheeks.

"We must leave soon. I know the guards are getting ready to comb every part of the city. I have to take you back to the oak trees before they get there. We can't risk them finding the mirror." Zac explained, his voice filled with pain.

"I'm going to miss you so much," Helena cried, holding Torvi's face in her hands.

"I will miss you too, Helena. You are a wonderful friend, and I'm glad I met someone like you," Torvi replied, her tears flowing faster.

They clung to each other and cried while Zac and Jason watched with tears in their eyes. When Helena and Torvi finally broke apart, Jason walked up to her and held her hands in his.

"I don't want to say goodbye, Torvi, but I guess I don't have a choice," he whispered, swallowing heavily. "I can't begin to thank you for everything you did. You saved me from my grief, restored my relationship with my sister, and helped me get her magic back. I will never forget you, and I will carry a memory of you in my heart wherever I go."

"Oh, Jason!" Torvi cried, unable to say anything more. She hugged him tightly, feeling as though her heart would burst from all the emotions churning through her.

"Goodbye, Torvi. You are a special friend I will always remember. Perhaps you will return soon, when Zac is our new master and the city is at peace again," Helena said after they broke apart. She gave Torvi one last hug before leaving the two lovers alone to say their goodbyes.

Torvi went into Zac's arms and wept, her shoulders trembling as he held her tightly. Burying his face in her hair, he rocked her back and forth until her cries subsided.

"I love you so much, Torvi," he whispered, kissing her hair.

"I love you too, Zac," she whimpered, tightening her arms around him.

Zac lifted her face, kissed her gently, and stared into her deep blue eyes.

"Torvi," he said, smiling at her. "You are the best thing that has ever happened to me, and I will cherish every memory we had together. You own my heart forever, and no one can replace you in my life. You're like my mirror, the other part of me, and you will always be my only true love," he confessed passionately, caressing her cheek.

"I feel exactly the same way, Zac," Torvi whispered, smiling through her tears. "The good times we had, I will always hold dear to my heart. This wonderful city will always be fresh in my mind. You are an amazing person, and I know you will be a great master, leading the people with justice and fairness."

"Thank you, Torvi. I will tell everyone in the city your story. You are our heroine. None of this would be possible if you hadn't come to our city. Now, I could stay talking to you until dawn, but I need to take you back," he chuckled, bending to kiss her lips again.

Torvi sighed deeply and nodded, "All right, let's go."

Outside, Torvi hugged Helena and Jason one last time. They stood waving at the sky as Zac took off with her, tears streaming down their faces.

Torvi clung to Zac's shoulders, gazing at the beautiful, glowing city below as they flew. Her heart ached, not knowing when she might see the city again. She couldn't believe she had only spent a few days there; it felt like a lifetime.

"Hold on tight, I can see some guards ahead, and I know they'll alert Fiya once they spot us. I'm going to fly faster so hold on tighter, okay?" Zac instructed.

"Okay," Torvi nodded, tightening her grip on him.

"There they are!" one of the guards shouted, pointing at them as they passed through the center of the city.

"Get Fiya now!" a voice commanded.

Torvi glanced down and saw that it was Caden. He looked like he wanted to fly after them. She resisted the urge to stick her tongue out at him as Zac flew past. Fiya appeared almost immediately, but they were already too far away for her to send her fire after them. She and the other guards began to run after them, and Torvi laughed at their futile attempts.

Soon, they reached the oak trees, and Zac set her down. She quickly spotted the tree with the mirror, marked by the cloak she had used to cover it.

"That tree over there," she said, pointing it out.

"I can't believe this," Zac gasped, staring at the tree.

"Can't believe what?" Torvi asked, looking up at him.

"I was here the exact day you arrived. I wanted a change of scenery and camped here for a day. That cloak is mine. I must have dropped it while leaving," Zac said, pointing at the tree.

"What a coincidence," Torvi chuckled, removing it from the mirror. "Your cloak helped me conceal the mirror!"

"I'm glad," Zac laughed. He was about to say something else when they heard footsteps behind them.

"You must go, now. They must have figured this place out. Go!" he urged, drawing her in for a brief kiss before pushing her toward the mirror.

Torvi nodded and stepped into the mirror. Fresh tears streamed down her cheeks as she turned to take one last look at Zac before disappearing completely.

In no time, she found herself back in the first room and she quickly ran to the window to look outside. It was nightfall, and the moon shone brightly in the sky.

Torvi stared down at the necklace Zac had given her and smiled, glad she had experienced the adventure of a lifetime.

1

About the Author

Celeste Devine is a hopeless romantic who delights in escapism from today's bustling world and ever-increasing demands on life. Her enchanting love stories draw readers into different realms, weaving fantasies and desires that captivate the heart. Celeste's writing is characterized by heartfelt emotion, relatable characters, and the belief that love knows no boundaries - transcending worlds, species, and time.

Born and raised in picturesque New Zealand, Celeste developed a passion for storytelling after years of immersing herself in various cultures, listening to their stories, and traveling to places vastly different from her own. After a fulfilling career in nursing, Celeste pursued her dream of becoming a writer. Her debut novel, *The Mystery of Ornate Mirrors: Magic Love*, quickly became a fan favorite. Her ambition is to guide readers through six journeys of forbidden love, lust, and adventure.

When she's not writing, Celeste enjoys exploring the scenic landscapes of New Zealand, indulging in a good cup of coffee, spending time with her beloved family and grandchildren, and pottering in her garden.

www.ingramcontent.com/pod-product-compliance
Lightning Source LLC
Chambersburg PA
CBHW071523150726
48000CB00002B/659